REVENGE INSTINCT?

AMIT DUBEY AND
RAVLEEN SABHARWAL

notionpress.com

INDIA · SINGAPORE · MALAYSIA

ISBN 979-8-88975-525-8

CONTENTS

PREFACE

"We spoil ourselves with scruples long as things go well."

Families are all different, and when families are in danger, all of them react differently. When the Chauhan family's loyal employee, Shiva Apte is attacked, the balance of the family shifts, towards something new. There is history that no one remembers, or no one is allowed to, and with Shiva Apte's death, all of them threaten to come spilling out onto the open. Families are forever, but the secret that ties the Chauhans, their rivals the Mehras, and their most loyal servant, Shiva, might just break them all apart.

Chapter 1

TROUBLE IN PARADISE

"A child not embraced by the village, will burn it down to feel its warmth."

– Hissar, Haryana, 1990

The big sugarcane field burns, lit up like Diwali, only that it isn't. The fields look more like a maze — impenetrable, and scary. The multiple gunshots ring out into the air, repeated gunshots breaking the peace of the night. The entire area surrounding the mansion was set ablaze, making it difficult to tell if the smoke was from the fire or from the multiple bombings that ensued. A political conflict, two opposing leading parties gnawing at each other.

A girl, of around 15 years, moved past the shooting and the incessant bloodshed. As she tried to run back into the outhouse, someone got a hold of her and swooped her in.

Delhi, 2020

A week ago, from present day

The Chauhan mansion, lit up with lights all around it. Each part of the giant house, brimming with blinding lights and shimmer. Ananya, the daughter of the third Chauhan brother, all set to be married in two weeks. This is a huge event in a family like that of the Chauhans. The giant gates are heavily guarded by security personnel who have been in service of the Chauhans for years on end. The city of Delhi all abuzz with the happenings at the Chauhan family wedding. Their influence came from Lata Diamonds, the brainchild of the Chauhan lineage, the largest jeweller in the market by far.

The preparations for the upcoming days were in full swing. There wasn't anybody who wasn't, in one way or the other, occupied with the wedding errands, running around either on calls, or supervising vendors and workers in the picturesque lawn. The wedding was supposed to be a day wedding, and the rituals would take place right beside the garden, in the middle of the lawn. The place smelled of fresh flowers and freshly baked bread, a waiter constantly running to and fro while Dushyant Chauhan, the father of the bride, sits down for breakfast.

Dressed in a beige kurta, and light sandals on his feet, he comes walking towards the lawn, to the *shamiyana*. His phone rings. "Ah, this is what I don't like. *Subah hone bhi nahi dete aur calls aa jatey hai.*" His annoyance with the work was palpable, and Ananya, the bride, decides to intervene.

"*Papa*, enough now. I'm asking you to sit down and have breakfast with us, and that is exactly what you are going to do."

Dushyant smiles and hangs up the call. "Anything for my *gudia*", he says. "What do we have for breakfast today?"

Ananya asks the waiter to let them be, and starts serving her father breakfast. Dushyant Chauhan was claimed to be the toughest among the five brothers of the Chauhan family, but then, his life changed forever after Ananya was born. This was one person he could not say no to, he would always, always comply. He loved her dearly, an only child.

As soon as he opened his mouth to say something to her, he saw Shiva running towards him, sticking his phone out. He frowned and stood up slowly. "Sss-sir", he fumbled. Ananya looked at him and exhaled.

"Kaam kaam aur kaam, aur kuch toh ata hi nahi hain aap logoko."

Shiva shook his head and interjected, *"Aisi baat nahi hai, bitiya. Ye* important *nahi hota, toh mai kabhi itni subah subah daura nahi aata. Mujhe bahut acche se pata hai ki ab priority sirf hamari* Ananya *hai."*

Ananya narrowed her eyes with a smile and said, "Okay, I will leave you for this time." She landed a soft kiss on her father's right cheek and said, "I will see you later."

After she was gone, Shiva said, "Sir, there's a call for you. They're saying it's urgent. The Mehra deal is off." A frown formed upon Dushyant's forehead. He quickly got off the table and rushed inside the house asking Shiva to wait. Shiva Apte basically ran the entire business operations and deals from the outside. Without him, nothing could be managed. All of them would call him 'Shiva *bhai*' but he was much older than them, in his 50s. He was a stout man, strongly built — the muscle of the family. He was the living proof that blood isn't the only element that binds a family. Though he wasn't technically a part of the Chauhan family, he had been with them for years now. Nothing, absolutely could go wrong in his presence.

As Dushyant started walking up the stairs, he crossed a whole corridor adorned with multiple business achievements and pictures of the family on both sides. The entire corridor smelled of fresh marigolds as they were placed on each railing staircase railing and along the pillars. At the end, was a teal grey door, and that is where Dushyant stopped. He waited there for a brief moment before he finally knocked. The door was opened.

"I was expecting you, *beta*", said his father, the head of this family and the business. Mr. Maan Singh Chauhan was the kingpin of this enormous diamond business, and has been running it for the past many years. He let Dushyant in. He seemed tense.

"What's the matter, Dad?" Dushyant asked, closing the door behind him.

Maan Singh sighed. "The Mehras have introduced new clauses right in the end, and for now the deal has been called off. You must do something."

Dushyant knew that the business meant more than anything else to their father in this world. He went towards the bed where his father was sitting and said, keeping his hand on Maan Singh's shoulders, "Don't worry, *bauji*. I'll make sure we don't end up on the losing side."

Maan Singh smiled and nodded.

Dushyant immediately left for the office and called a meeting to set up a new deal. What ensued was a gruelling session between the two parties, either of who refused to give up. It came to a point where they would have lost the deal, right when Dushyant's brother, Anshul entered the office.

"Excuse me, gentlemen. I'm sorry for being late. Delhi traffic, huh," Anshul took a seat, "So, the original deal was to close in on us taking 25% equity, and we don't see any reason to lower our bargain than that."

"But we have a growing company, why would we be selling that much equity to you?"

He scoffed. "With due respect, your company is far from growing. You have incurred huge losses since last year, and that is why this whole deal is being made. But you chose to turn it around in your favour by making us think that by investing in you, we are getting a good deal, which we're clearly not. If anything, we're doing you a favour. So, come to terms with our conditions and we all can go home happy."

Dushyant stood there and watched his brother, crack an impossible deal with ease.

They shook hands and the client left.

He looked back at Dushyant and said, "Research, dig up things and you can have any deal you want. Problem solved, now we can go back home. C'mon, we have a wedding to prepare for!"

The oldest born, Anshul Chauhan, is a person to look up to. Smart, full of grit for his passion, business. Some even say that he is the only one in the family to have truly imbibed Maan Singh's business capabilities.

Once the brothers walked back to the *shamiyana* the preparations were in full swing. The vendors, housekeepers and managing teams — all were present at the venue. Anshul dived right into the preparations.

Anshul went straight to their father's room where his father was waiting impatiently. This was a big deal, and he had saved it single-handedly. As he heard the knock on his door, a faint smile formed on his lips. He knew it was Anshul, and nothing could go wrong if it was in his hands. He opened the door to see Anshul standing out front, victory etched on his face.. Maan Singh was all praises for his eldest son, who had proved his merit in the business yet again. Dushyant was not far behind Anshul, he walked right into the room hoping their father would be angry…but seeing him smile, Dushyant heaved a sigh of relief. "I'll call the caterer. He's not been doing his job properly. The menu samples have not even arrived!"

Anshul interrupted, "Don't worry about it. I've called them already and very specifically informed them that if they don't take this job seriously, we can find someone else. They will be arriving with the samples very soon.".

"Ah yes, that's my son. Working his way around everything", said Maan Singh, almost hinting that Dushyant wasn't capable enough. Dushyant's face dropped a little, but he seemed to gather himself up quickly enough. He rushed out of the room hearing his wife, Damini, calling out for him.

Anshul also took Maan Singh's leave and left the room. Damini was an exemplary woman — gold medal in physics — but those times called for different fates for women. She fell prey to it too and got married off to Dushyant, marking the end of her career. Over the years, she tried to pick her pieces up bit by bit, trying to help out in the business, where elaborate discussions with Anshul Chauhan led to fruitful decisions. It was sad how a person like her would now only be known as a socialite, blending into the norms that the superficial society assigns to trophy wives. The worst part was her awareness, her awareness, of deserving something better. that she somewhere knows deep down that she deserved better. Even though she was one of the younger ones in the family, it was safe to say that she was running the household after the untimely demise of Anshul's wife, Mrs. Kamala Chauhan. Since then, she has kept the family together and running.

Ananya was sitting on the terrace as her designer and stylist surrounded her, with what felt like constant blabbering to her about what she needed to wear and how things needed to be. Ananya's eyes were fixated on her phone. From time to time, she would try to take a quick glance at it. The trials started, and she was made to wear multiple outfits to find the perfect ones for her wedding rituals. In the middle of all this, her phone buzzed. She ran towards it like a kid. Taking it up in her hand, she sighed, her face glooming with disappointment. She kept it down on the table, this time, putting it on silent mode, like she didn't want to know anymore. The trials went on for some more time. There were too many options, themes, shades, to choose from. All she wanted was to keep things simple. Despite knowing that coming from an influential family as hers come with certain restrictions and liberties one cannot take, she wanted to believe she could have something different. She was not ready to face the world how her family wants to, she wants to do it her way. While she was immersed in all of these thoughts, one of the house helps knocked on the terrace door to ask if they could let the guest in, only, it wasn't a guest. Ananya's eyes lit up as she made her way to the door. She hugged the person the moment she was close enough.

"This is not fair, you've been gone since last night…not answering any of my calls or texts. Where have you been, Sooraj?" she asked, burying her face in his chest.

He cupped her face in his hands and rested his lips on her forehead for a brief second. He gazed at her and said, "Baby, I was right here. Just got a little busy with work you know, just the usual. Had to be in Noida for a night. Hurried back here as soon as the work got done. See, I'm here now!"

The frown on Ananya's face was fading away a little, her squinted eyes coming back to normal, pupils dilated at the sight of the person that she was dying to see for hours. Sooraj was Ananya's fiance. A self-made man, with mind-boggling revenues to his business. Sooraj Rathi had become a name, unavoidable in the business sector all over Delhi and NCR. His success story was that of sheer grit and perseverance and one that nobody could ignore. Ananya and Sooraj had stumbled upon each other at the club for the first time. That is how they met, and what ensued is epic history.

"Hey, you're here. Why didn't you let us know?" said Dushyant walking in on them.

Ananya pulled herself away when she heard her father's voice.

"I-I hadn't planned to exactly be here right now but…"

"But what? I understand *beta*, it gets hard to stay away especially when the wedding is so near. You jump at every little chance you get to spend time with your partner. I get it."

Sooraj smiled a little, didn't say anything though. He was many things, but not exactly outgoing. When it came to situations like these, he would seem shy.

Ananya intervened, *"Papa*, let him be *na,* he's here to see me, and we're going on a drive. Right now. I'm fed up with these preparations and managing everything for the wedding."

Dushyant smiled as his eyes travelled to Sooraj, expecting him to say something.

He didn't disappoint. "Yes, we have the rest of the days to just work on these things only, but for today, let me steal her for a while. She needs some fresh air, I believe."

"Of course, *beta*. I understand. You go, we have time for the rest." Dushyant concurred.

Ananya grabs Sooraj's hand, and walks straight out of the room. The family had never seen Ananya this chirpy, she was always quite reserved. But, she was a whole new person around Sooraj. Once they got into the car, she asked, "Where are we going?"

"Let's see where the road takes us…."

"But…

"It's a surprise, baby."

A faint smile forms on Ananya's lips. This was the happiest she has ever been in her life. They drove past Delhi, crossing the city lines. Ananya was surprised, she had no clue where he was taking her. Finally, after a 2.5-hour long drive, they reached a resort. The place was a little hilly. Little did Ananya know that Sooraj had planned out a whole surprise for her at the villa. She was overjoyed at what all was being done for her. Right when they were about to sit down to eat, Ananya got a call from Dushyant. His voice was shaking.

"*Papa*, what's wrong? What happened?" she asked, bringing her eyebrows together.

"*Beta*, come home fast, just come."

Ananya knew something was up. She immediately asked Sooraj to drive her back. On the way back, there wasn't a single moment when Ananya was not freaking out. She kept looking at her phone in the hope of maybe getting another call or text. One thing Ananya could not live with is not knowing things or things being kept from her. Her palms were sweaty, and she felt short of breath. Sooraj tried to rub her palms, but all in vain. She had acute anxiety, as diagnosed quite a few years back.

She hadn't felt like this quite some time and now that she was, she did not know what to do. Sooraj being in her life, changed a lot of things. Her mental health got better alongside other things. As they reached Delhi and were entering their mansion's gate. They saw the police standing outside with an ambulance parked right in front. Ananya's panic knew no bounds at that point. She rushed down the car, followed by a concerned Sooraj. As they rushed inside the mansion, they saw that it was full of people — security personnel and there was chaos everywhere. Ananya rushed to Dushyant and asked, "Are you alright? I was worried sick about you."

She was almost on the verge of crying. Dushyant's face looked upset and scared at the same time. "Shiva…he…he was attacked…he's being taken to the ICU."

"What?" Ananya couldn't believe her ears.

"We don't know what happened but one of the housekeepers found him lying unconscious and bleeding on the terrace. Nobody would have found him also had they not gone to clean the terrace post your fittings. There was a lot of blood, as if he was dragged from somewhere else and placed there. The chances of him surviving seem grim right now. We don't know what happened."

Ananya, at this point, could not gauge the severity of the situation anymore. She had grown up in this house, and thought it was impenetrable. But now, she felt unsafe for the first time in her life. Shiva, the person she had always thought of as part of the household, had been taken to the ICU. Ananya and Dushyant decided to leave for the hospital as soon as possible. Sooraj stayed back to talk to the police and handle things.

On the way to the hospital, they were following the ambulance as Ananya kept weeping. Her anxiety was over the roof. Dushyant kept asking her to calm down, but he knew about the sheer trauma that the whole family would go through. Soon after, Ananya could see Sooraj's car following them. In Ananya's distressed state, Sooraj was the only person who could help her.

They reached the hospital and rush towards the ICU. The operation wasn't over yet. Shiva suffered internal bleeding, and the doctors were not being able to say anything yet. The Chauhan family was quite concerned about Shiva as he had been with them for a long time now. He was family. Dushyant was only talking to the other family members when Anshul walked in. His boots tapping on the floor could be heard from quite afar in the otherwise quiet hospital corridor. Ananya respected Anshul a lot, and was quite his favourite. Anshul rushed in and Ananya hugged him, tight. "Did you get to know who did this to Shiva *bhaiya*?" Anshul's face had disappointment on it, but then, him being him, did not flinch. He had a faint smile on his lips, and said "Don't worry, *beta*. We will find the culprit and punish him. Shiva will be fine, I believe."

Sooraj walked into the hospital now, and Ananya went and sat by his side. He offered to bring her coffee, which she denied. "It's 12.30 in the night, and you haven't had food…at least have the coffee." he said.

"Sooraj, the coffee might help with the tiredness but it makes me hyper…and I don't want that. I don't want to feel so much right now, a few weeks away from the wedding…I cannot believe this is how we're going to start our new lives."

Anshul asked one of the doctors treating Shiva, if he will be okay or if he is out of danger now. To which, the doctor just nodded off, indicating that nothing could be said yet again. After a whole hour of loitering in the hospital corridor, the doctor came out and said one of them could come inside. Shiva could not even move or say anything properly. But he was more stable than before. Anshul went in, Shiva tried grabbing his hand, trying to say something.

Anshul said, "Shiva…who did this to you?"

Shiva groaned… "He…hit…me….please…"

Before he could finish the sentence, he fell unconscious, gasping for breath. Whatever he said, sounded like gibberish to Anshul. The doctor barged in and asked Anshul to leave, and not exhaust the patient anymore. The internal bleeding and the sheer blood loss was making him weak, and he was fading in and out.

Ananya was sent home around 3 in the morning, and as she was walking upstairs and crossed Shiva's room…she felt like she was someone inside. She looked in again. Nobody was there. She was about to walk away, but something stopped her. There was a big photograph of all the Chauhan brothers along with Shiva on the wall just outside Shiva's room.

Ananya froze.

She could not speak a word, and then suddenly, she cried out loud. Everybody woke up, and ran upstairs. What they saw, they couldn't believe. Ananya was on the floor, curled up with her face cupped in her hands. She was terrified. On that photograph, Shiva's face had been scratched out with some sort of a black marker. They could not figure out what it was, but it triggered Ananya's anxiety.

This is right when Ananya got a call from Anshul, saying that Shiva was no more.

Chapter 2

A DEATH IN THE FAMILY

"Appearance tyrannises over truth"

– Plato

It was the first time in a while that somebody had died in the family. There was grief and while the whole situation would have been different otherwise, it was still a few days till the big wedding. Ananya was sitting in a corner, clad in white, like the rest of them, biting her nails.

She couldn't remove that image from her mind. Every time she closes her eyes, that is all she sees. That figure in the room. It was real. What if she had gone in a little earlier? Could she catch him? Would she have been able to?

What if she had screamed for help earlier? Would it have made a difference?

She shook her head off, trying to declutter her mind, putting these thoughts to rest for some time.

"Hey." She heard somebody from behind. She didn't turn to understand who it was. She closed her eyes and exhaled like somebody lifted a stone off of her chest.

"Where were you, Sooraj?", she groaned.

Sooraj came and sat behind her, landing a soft peck in her cheek. She rested her head on his shoulder. He smiled, holding her close.

"Doesn't matter. What matters is that I am here now."

"I just can't stop thinking about it, Sooraj."

She lifted her head and looked at him, with a grimace on her face. "I just can't stop", she murmured.

He frowned and said, "What do you mean?"

"That day. I saw him. I saw him. Only if I was there a tad bit earlier."

She stopped and gazed at her feet. She reached into his hands and asked, "Do you think I could have seen his face? Do you think I-"

Sooraj covered her mouth with the palm of his hand. "Enough", he said, smiling. He removed his hand and continued, "I understand the situation is too strenuous for you right now but let's try to remember what the therapist told you."

He looked at her, raising his eyebrows, anticipating a response from her.

She crooked her nose.

"You can't...", Sooraj trailed off, bobbing his so that she catches up to him midway.

She doesn't disappoint. "You can't control the past", she said.

"That's right."

"Do you think he'll get caught?"

He laughed a little, looking at her. He exhaled and said, as the smile lingered on his face, "I do believe that justice will be served."

He scanned her face and said, "You've been through a lot."

He put an arm around her shoulder and said, "All these wedding preparations are only adding to the pressure. Why can't we just leave all of this behind and run away?"

She smiled. "When will you grow up, Sooraj?" She untwined her hands from his and said, "A part of me still wishes if that could be possible in my wildest dreams but-"

She stands up, her back towards him. "It's not possible. Not as long as I am part of the Chauhan lineage. I can't do that to my family."

She turned towards him, putting her hand forward. He held her hand and got up. As he inched closer, she put up a wide smile. So wide, that it lacked credibility.

"And we both know that I have to accept that there's no escaping *that*."

"You don't have to", he said, tugging a stand of her hair behind her ears. "I'm here now. We'll get married and then, we'll build a life of our own."

"This will still be a part of my identity, Sooraj. I cannot just flee my responsibilities. I-"

"What are you two love birds doing in the corner?", a voice interrupted.

It was her cousin Ashish, her father's older brother Angad's only son. She is closer to him than most of her other brothers - mostly because they were born a day apart.

"You guys have no shame, do you? Somebody just died in the house and you two! Tch tch tch", he teased them, shaking his head.

Ananya hit his arm playfully. "Your tongue doesn't know when or where to stop. *Kuch bhi, haan*? We were just talking."

Ashish held up both of his hands, sniggering. "Don't explain to me. I'm not the one who is looking for you."

"Who is looking for me?" she inquired.

"Dushyant *chachu*. Who else?"

"I'll be right back", she whispered to Sooraj and hurried off.

Ashish looked at him and said, "Go, follow her. She's not the only one he is looking for."

Sooraj widened his eyes as he lifted a finger, pointing a finger at himself. "Me?" he asked.

"Yep, now go on."

He went after her to see the both of them standing at the stairs. He slowed his pace and stopped in front of him.

Sooraj smiled at Dushyant as he nodded. "As you can understand, the situation isn't too good right now. The loss of Shiva is more than any of us could fathom. He was an indispensable part of not just the company but also our family. It will take us a lot of time to get back to normal, to accept them it will be normal without him."

He paused for a minute. He sighed and said, "We all have been very busy the past few days for the wedding and as soon as we are done with his crematory service, we will have to dive right back into it. In any case, I want some help from you kids. Could you please go and meet the police for the time being? SP Ramanujan will be waiting for you. I will catch up with him soon enough but-"

"Don't worry, Papa. Sooraj and I will meet him. It won't be a problem", Ananya intervened. She looked at Sooraj, expecting him to join in.

He knew the look. "Yes, sir, err-I mean, *papa*."

They laughed, and Ananya said, "He'll take some time with that one."

Dushyant patted on his back and said, "Take all the time you want, *beta*. I am not going anywhere."

With that, Dushyant left the courtyards. Ananya looked at him and giggled. "Yes, sir- I mean, *papa*", she ridiculed.

He covered his face with his hands in embarrassment. "Oh my god", a muffled voice came out of him.

"Chalo, thik hai, koi nahi. It's not that big of a deal. Not like you said it to somebody you'd have to maintain a relationship with for the rest of your life."

He looked at her flatly.

"Oops", she said, before breaking out into laughter.

"You're the worst, man", he said, taking the keys out of his pocket.

They walked to the garage and he took his car out.

"You wanna drive?" Sooraj suggested, looking at her.

"Yeah, sure", she said, a little hesitantly.

They drove to the police station where, like Dushyant had said, SP Ramanujan was waiting for them. He was standing in front of the station, talking to another one of his colleagues. He shared a longstanding relationship with the Chauhans and knew Ananya quite well too.

When he saw her get off the car, he appeared a little confused.

"I wasn't expecting you. What are you doing here?"

Ananya stopped. She tilted her head a little and said, "Are you saying that I shouldn't have been here?"

Ramanujan laughed nervously, shaking his head. "No, no. Not what I meant. It's just that I usually expect your father or uncles to be here."

"Well, they are busy with everything that has happened… all you'll get today is me. Does that work for you?"

He laughed and nodded. His focus shifted to Sooraj who was standing right next to her. He pointed towards him and said, "And who's that?"

"Oh", Ananya said, grabbing Sooraj's arm. "That's the person lucky enough to get married to me."

"Hmm." Ramanujan eyed Sooraj, "welcome to the family."Sooraj smiled and nodded. "Let's go inside now. We can start talking about what you have discovered till now."

"Absolutely," Ramanujan replies, leading them to his office, "while I cannot be certain, initial investigations point to this being the work of hired killers. There have been little to none in the way of evidence."

"The time window was also too short for anyone to make an escape without alerting the security," Sooraj offers helpfully, "all of them were in the house at that time. Except for us."

"Ah yes, newlyweds-to-be." The inspector's face softens, only for a second, "I believe someone may have been hired to injure Shiva Apte, or to kill him outright. They didn't have enough time to finish the job, so they dragged him to the terrace and left him there to be found."

"They thought that he would be dead by the time we found him." Ananya supplies the end, burying her face in her hands, "what have we done?"

"The post-mortem report has the details in full," Inspector Ramanujan says, "he died due to blunt force trauma to the head, which resulted in loss of blood. There were signs of a struggle, but no DNA was discovered from his body, and the murder weapon has also not been discovered."

"Essentially, we are at a dead end, then." Ananya says softly, "none of this would have happened if we hadn't left the house. Shiva would still be here, and we wouldn't be at the police station, trying to find out who killed *bhaiya*."

None of them had anything to say to that. Ananya was wrong, her words coming from a place of abject grief, but didn't they all think the same? The Chauhans had been broken by the death of their family member. Every day, someone refused to eat food, and the wedding preparations were all but stopped. Neither Sooraj nor Ananya had any interest in getting married anymore, continuing only out of duty.

"The guilt of Shiva Apte's death lies upon his murderer, not his bereaved family," Inspector Ramanujan begins in a matter-of-fact tone. "don't worry about the rest of the formalities. I will keep your family updated of the progress of this case. Rest assured, you will find us to be entirely cooperative."

The pair walked out of the police station, hand in hand, and Ananya asked, "will they be able to find whoever killed bhaiya?"

"Why do you call him that?" Sooraj asked, leading her into the car, "your father and his brothers call him *bhaiya* too. And so do you. Isn't it a bit weird?"

"You've come over to my house so many times, and yet I can't believe you never asked me about this until now,"

Ananya says with a wry smile, "it's been a habit. I've seen the people in my house call him *bhaiya* all the time, and in my mind, only older, respectable people get called *bhaiya*. So I adopted the honourific, even though I really didn't need to. My parents were not very happy when they heard me call him by his name."

"I think it's cute."

"You think everything is cute." Ananya grins, "I think my mom and dad are waiting for us now. They've already called me twice."

ଔ◈ଛ

As expected, Dushyant was eagerly awaiting the return of his daughter and his son-in-law. Although, he supposes, he really shouldn't call him his son-in-law already. That would be presumptuous of him. no matter the preparations that had been done, neither Ananya nor Sooraj were married, by law or by faith. And yet, he couldn't stop thinking of the reliable young man as his son-in-law already.

Ah, it's just the wedding, Dushyant Chauhan tells himself, they are going to be married in only a few days. And then, there will be no need to be so distant with Sooraj. We can formally accept him into the family.

The car rolls up into the driveway, and Dushyant finds himself walking out to greet the two of them, a small smile on his face. Ananya practically jumps out of the car, running to him, and even from a distance, he can see the smile on Sooraj's face. *Good. Ananya chose well.*

He leads them into the house, and once theyre seated comfortably on the sofa, Dushyant begins, "What did Inspector Ramanujan say? Is there any new information on who could have killed Shiva? Are they any close to finding out the truth?"

"Papa," Sooraj says softly, after Dushyant had stopped to catch a breath, "we do have information."

"Let us speak, at least." Ananya grumbles from beside him, and Sooraj gestures her to stop, "what? I'm right. *Papa,* we can't really tell you everything that we have learnt, if you keep talking like this, without even taking a breath."

"I see," Dushyant laughs, "well, I'll stop for now. But *beta,* you need to tell me. your grandfather is already very anxious."

The both nod, and Sooraj begins, 'Inspector Ramanujan thinks it was done by a professional. He told us that the time within which the fatal attack had happened, was too short for an unplanned attack. Whoever is behind it, they had enough time to prepare for all possibilities. They knew when Ananya would have her trials, and that the terrace would be deserted after they left. It was all planned extremely meticulously, with very little room for error. And clearly, they didn't make an error."

Dushyant sighs, leaning back into the sofa. *So, they had planned it all.* He had held out the hope for it to be a work of someone amateur, someone who had made mistakes, someone who would be caught easily. At least then, he wouldn't feel the overwhelming guilt of potentially facilitating the murder of one of his most trusted associates. He cannot sleep at night. His nightmares are inconsistent, but they come by, without fail.

And in all of them, he is rendered immobile. He, the second son of the Chauhan family, he is unworthy of all the respect that they bestow upon him, because who is he, if he cannot protect his family? Shiva was a part of their family, and he had allowed for this to happen.

The footsteps enter the room, and he holds his head in his hands. *I cannot do this anymore.* He feels guity for letting his daughter and her not-yet husband go in his stead, ashamed to even face the inspector.

"Ah, *maa,*" Ananya says, and Sooraj stands up. "Sooraj and I were just talking about what Inspector Ramanujan had told us."

Damayanti sighs. Dushyant doesn't blame her. None of them were prepared for this. Least of all, Sooraj and Ananya. *But look at them, taking it all in their stride.* "Inspector Ramanujan said that this was most likely the work of someone experienced."

Dushyant does not even need to look at Damini to know that her face is set in a hard frown, as she contemplates the future of their family. *Murder and a wedding. I wonder what people think of us now.* Ananya starts talking again. He barely hears anything.

"Are you okay?" his wife's voice breaks through the reverie, and Dushyant drags himself out of his thoughts, "you kept looking out into the distance."

"Nevermind," Dushyant stands up, and turning to Ananya and Sooraj, says, stiffly, "I'll call for lunch."

Ananya looks confused, "are you not going to join us for lunch?"

Dushaynt shakes his head, "no, *beta.* I have to meet with Dad now. He has been asking for news from the police station for the past few days, and all I've been able to tell him isnt nearly enough to satisfy him."

Sooraj cracks a small smile, but Ananya giggles loudly. Damini simply nods her head at him.

The portraits on the hallways are all covered, and there is a large blank patch where the family portrait used to occupy pride of place. He shudders. Once, twice. And then, knocks on the door leading to his father's room.

"Come in," his father says, voice loud enough to be carried over the thick doors. His father is looking over some papers, glasses set over his nose. In a flash, Dushyant is reminded of his own childhood, waiting for his father to finish work, the anticipation of a reprimand. He always feels like a little child in front of his father. No matter how well-respected and revered Dushyant Chauhan became, in front of his father, he would still be that seven-year old boy, terrified of a beating.

"What did Inspector Ramanujan say?"

"They think it was done by someone experienced. Most likely, they knew about the days' itinerary, and attacked Shiva Apte when they knew he would be alone, and we would not be paying attention." The words come out of Dushyant in a rush, but his father looks at him approvingly. *Ah, right. I shouldn't be so dependant on my father's praise. He never gives it away freely.*

"I will talk to Inspector Ramanujan," Maan Sing says, "focus on Ananya's wedding for now. There weren't too many people hired for the event. If we look into them all, we can surely find a solution."

"We should send the list of all the employees hired specifically for the wedding, to the police," Dushyant interjects, voice weaker than he would have liked it to be. "The police would appreciate it."

"And we will," his father insists, placing his hand atop a thick, heavy folder, "but not before we, as a family, look at what had happened that day. As a family, the Chauhans are humiliated now, the happy occasion of Ananya's wedding turned into a funeral instead."

Dushyant doesn't say anything. *What is there to say, when the man is right?* The security of their house, as well as that of his family, was up to them. they had failed on both counts. The joy of Ananya's wedding had gone, replaced with a funereal atmosphere. No one smiled anymore, other than Ananya. Least of all, Dushyant. *No one can understand why this happened. No one even knows if the wedding guests will give their blessings to Ananya. Our reputation is ruined, especially with a police investigation taking place in the house where there should be a wedding.*

"Absolutely," he murmurs, "shall we hire someone to look into the matters of the new hires?"

"There is no need for that," Maan Singh replies, "you and Anshul can take care of it."

Dushyant merely nods. Once his father had made up his mind, there was very little that anyone could do to change it.

He walked out of the room, closing the heavy doors behind him, and coming face-to-face with Anshul.

"I heard everything from Ananya," his older brother says, "did father call you?"

"It was most likely an inside job," Dushyant replies, "father told you and me to look into the thing, together."

"Before informing the police?" Anshul raises an eyebrow, "shouldn't we give up all information to the police?"

That's exactly what I was trying to say, Dushyant thinks, "father thinks that we may be able to save face if we could apprehend the attacker before the police get more involved in this."

"I understand," Anshul tilts his head, "wedding guests are cancelling. The gossip tabloids have had a field day with this horrible, horrible incident."

"The only person who could have smoothed things over, was Shiva," Dushyant muses, "and he is no longer here."

Chapter 3

FAMILY

"It takes something more than intelligence, to act intelligently."

– Fyodor Dostoevsky

"Are you supposed to be doing all this? Ananya is going to get married in three days, and now you have to go through with this wild-goose chase?" Damini asks, the frustration evident in her voice, "we should not be investigating the attack, we should hand it over to the police. We aren't detectives we neither have the resources, nor the abilities to do this."

She's fuming. Dushyant sighs. There was only so much that he could do, short of explicitly going against his father, and causing a rift within the family. "Its late, Damini," he tries to soothe her, "we can think about all this tomorrow."

"You are holding the folder of all the people that were newly hired for the wedding," she argues, "Shiva *bhaiya* had hired all of them personally. Your older brother was responsible for hiring everyone, but Shiva took over from him, saying that he should do this much at least, for Ananya's wedding. And one of the people that Shiva *bhaiya* hired, killed him."

Dushyant sits up straighter in the chair, focusing all his attention on his wife, "are you sure? Anshul-*bhaiya* had told us all that he would be the one to hire the extra help needed. But it was Shiva?"

Damini huffs. "I overheard them talking. Shiva *bhaiya* told your brother—" and here she looks contrite, "—that he would take over the hiring process, since all of you were busy with the investment deal and too busy to make any preparations for Ananya's wedding. I know I shouldn't have eavesdropped, but they really were not having a private conversation."

"They were in a hallway, discussing this?"

"I don't think they thought the matter of any importance," Damini replies, flicking the bedside lamp's switch, and the room is suddenly immersed in a curious sort of half-darkness, where Dushyan cannot make out the profile of his wife, but is keenly aware of her presence. "They were both very casual about it." Damini finishes speaking, and Dushyant wonders if he had missed out on something extremely important.

"There should be a record of all the people he hired, then," he says, "Shiva was fastidious about keeping records, of everything. I'm sure he has a list somewhere."

"Is that the file?" Damini questions, and Dushyant can see only her silhouette, sitting upright in bed, "did *Papa* give you this?"

"Yes," Dushyant nods, "these are Shiva's accounts of everything that he had done for us. The list of people he had hired, must be in here."

Damini raches for the bedside lamp, flicking it on, "tell me then."

Dushyant opens the file, leafing through all its contents. Shiva had been a meticulous note-taker; every work that he had done for the Chauhan family, he had documented. Nothing was out of place. Except.

"The list isnt here," Dushyant says, dazedly, "the list of people is supposed to be here, and it just—it disappeared."

"I'm sure the pages are there. Look over it once more." Dushyant nods at his wife's words, and goes over the pages once again, but to no avail. The clock read one in the morning. "No, nothing here."

"Then the pages should be in Shiva-*bhaiya's* room, in his desk." Damini says, "you'll just have to wait until tomorrow, to get the papers. He may have kept it somewhere else, for easy access during the wedding."

"Father had been talking to him a lot," Dushyant muses, pulling out another paper, "this is an invoice, filed for his car's gas bill. Refunded by the company, Lata Diamonds. A bill for fifty thousand rupees, over two months."

"*Fifty thousand?* Where was father sending him to?" Dushyant's own mind had echoed the same question, but his wife had articulated it. "And you didn't know?"

Dushyant shakes his head, "no, I did not. If I had known, then this would not have been a surprise to me. I'm just as in the dark as you are."

Damini frowns, "and Shiva-*bhaiya* didn't tell you either, did he?"

"No."

Damini thinks for a moment, and Dushyant can see the cogs in her mind turning. Damini was an exceptional woman, much, much more intelligent than he was. He did not mind leaving this sleuthing to her in the slightest. "Well," she begins, staring off into the distance, "you cannot bring this to either your father, nor your brothers."

"Why?"

"If *Papa* hadn't told you about this, then it means Shiva-*bhaiya* was doing something for him, that he didn't want anyone to know, not even his own children." She finishes, "you need to go about this on your own."

Dushyant nods. But from the look of distress that had flitted across Damini's face, he knew that her thoughts were exactly the same as his own.

What if the work that Shiva-bhaiya was doing for his father, got him killed?

È◆৽

Inspector Ramanujan was, by all means, a clever man. He had maintained a good working relationship with all the high-profile families under his jurisdiction, including the chauhans of Lata Diamonds, and the other prominent jewellers of the city, all of whom were in intense competition with one another. For Lata Diamonds, it was not a case of occuoying more territory, they were already the leading jewellers of the entire Delhi-NCR area. It was a matter of holding onto their territory. The Mehras, of Mehra Jewellers, have been impatiently waiting to grab onto every lost territory of Lata Diamonds. Capturing every bit of the market share that they could. Inspector Ramanujan knew all about this. One didn't have to be Sherlock Holmes to retain basic information. He knew the Mehras, and he knew the Chauhans. He never told them about each other, however. It isn't my business, he reasoned, if they want to destroy each other in the quest for more influence and money, then so be it.

This morning, he had called on the Chauhan family patriarch, Maan Singh Chauhan. His youngest daughter-in-aw, Damini Chauhan had led him to her father-in-law's office, and had only reappeared to set a tray of food in front of him.

And of course, he had been waiting alone for the duration of his visit. Maan Singh had not yet made an appearance, and the only reason that he had been given, again by the daughter-in-law, was so shoddy that he had seen through it in an instant.

"Ah, there you are!" Maan Singh's voice was jovial, too much for it to be natural. Inspector Ramanujan extends a hand, bypassing the outstretched arms of the Chauhan family patriarch. For his part, Maan Singh does not look offended, and even if he is, which Ramanujan suspects him to be (all the tabloid coverage cannot be comfortable for them) he does not say anything, simply shaking his hands, and settles down in the chair.

"Well, should we cut to the chase?" Ramanujan is impatient, his gestures evident. "The police needs to search Mr Shiva Apte's room. In addition to this, we require the list of new hires for the wedding of Ms Ananya Chauhan."

Maan Singh looks at him for a second. Ramanujan feels, awkwardly, that he was in a situation, where it was certainly not to his advantage. It is an odd sensation, of being observed, much like the way a predator observes his prey. He wonders, idly, if he has given much of his cards away. Never mind. I can always deal over again. I am the dealer in this poker game.

Finally, Maan Singh laughed, and the tension in the room thickened, instead of relaxing, "I always liked you, Inspector. Who else would demand things, instead of being polite with me?"

"It is my duty," Ramanujan replies, gritting his teeth. Hopefully, Maan Singh would not notice it, "withholding information from the police is a criminal offence, Mr Chauhan. I hope you are aware of it."

"As are you, I believe," Maan Singh says, before calling, "Anshul!"

Almost on cue, the eldest Chauhan brother walks into the room, far too smoothly for Ramanujan's liking, "Anshul," Maan Singh's voice is softer now, like velvet, wrapped around the steel barrel of a revolver, "hand me the list of all the people Shiva hired for the wedding, specifically."

"Yes, Papa," Anshul produces a large manila folder, handing it to Ramanujan without a single word of protest, "here, Inspector."

Inspector Ramanujan takes the offered file, and gives it a cursory glance. Nothing out of the ordinary, although he would not put it past the Chauhans to withhold information from him. No matter the threat of the law, I suspect the shame is greater. "Shiva Apte's phone was obtained among his personal belongings. His phone records have been checked."

Maan Singh pales for a moment, immediately regaining his composure. "What did you find in there?" he asks, and Ramanujan almost scoffs at his face. Beside Maan Singh, Anshul Chauhan bristles, but like his father, his expression too, is gone within a minute.

"That is for the police to know, Mr Chauhan," he replies smoothly, "we will remain in touch. All of you will be required to provide a statement at the police station."

"Of course," Anshul Chauhan says faintly, "absolutely."

"I will take my leave now," Inspector Ramanujan stands up, tucking the file underneath his arm, "have a good day."

Inspector Ramanujan places a hand on the door, and turns back to face both Maan Sing and Anshul Chauhan, who have both donned their impervious mask of politeness, "oh, and before I forget, no one of this family is allowed to leave the city, until the investigation is complete."

The heavy doors close after him with a resounding thud.

On the car ride back to the police station, Inspector Ramanujan looks through the file of people that Shiva Apte had hired. Only one stands out. He makes a phone call.

"SI Alam," he says into the phone, "bring the Chauhans into the station tomorrow, to record their statements."

"Yes, sir," the slightly distorted voice of his immediate junior flows over the phone, "we were supposed to be waiting until Ananya Chauhan's wedding, but I'll push the dates to tomorrow."

"Do that," Inspector Ramanujan says, "I do not trust that family an inch. They have something to hide, and they are doing a bang-up job of it."

"Not necessarily a good one," his subordinate quips, "a man has died."

"God knows how many men have died," Ramanujan murmurs, "also, bring Aditya Mehra, of Mehra Jewellery, over to the station tomorrow. We need to know why a distant cousin of the Mehra family's 'right-hand man' was hired at a Chauhan wedding."

"Will do, Sir."

"Look into it, Alam, look into it," Ramanujan mutters, disconnecting the call. This is shaping up to become a very bad week for me. First, the murder of an important employee of one of the most powerful families in Delhi. Second, the Chauhans' reluctance to provide anything of importance. Sure, they have given us permission to search their entire household, but without a proper search warrant, all of that is useless. And the judge is being an asshole. Wonder who has him in their pockets. Is it the Chauhans? But how would they benefit by withholding information about the death of their own trusted steward?

Unless of course, the murder was done on their orders. Ramanujan would not put it past the family, neither would he put it past any of their rivals. Delhi and its upper-class society were full of families like this, who would think nothing of getting rid of their most loyal employees, as though it meant nothing to them. sure, they went on and on about how they were 'family', but when it came to the real thing—blood came before all else.

So, what exactly was Shiva doing, that got him killed? If he had been murdered by an amateur, a case of a murder of passion, there would have been more evidence left, owing simply to the very little time that they had, in between Ananya Chauhan's time on the terrace, and the time of death, and only forty-five minutes before the body was discovered. Roughly only an hour. And he had been killed somewhere else, his body moved to the terrace, left to be discovered by the family. If it had been a crime done on the spur of the moment, even if it had been premeditated, the assailant wouldn't have had so much experience, arranging the body to be discovered by the immediate family.

Almost as a message.

Inspector Ramanujan presses the phone to his ears, "Alam? Do we have the warrant yet?"

"The judge has said that he will sign it," the other officer explains, "I expect he will give it to us at the end of the day, just to anger us even more. The more time he wastes, the better for him."

"Do we have the call logs from Shiva Apte's phone?" Ramanujan asks, slightly irritated, "the judge keeps on delaying things, and we can't get a hold of anything if we do not have a warrant."

"We do have the call logs, sir," Alam says, hesitating for a while, "but there was nothing out of the ordinary, other than the calls made to the people that he had hired. All we could find were calls made to the executives at Lata Diamonds, and those are all pretty harmless. They were planning to release a new collection of bridal jewellery, later this year. Ananya Chauhan was supposed to wear the latest collection for her wedding."

"A wedding collection? Well, I suppose that would make sense. The marriage of the Chauhan daughter to Sooraj Rathi has been the first thin on every tabloid these days." Ramanujan mutters, "still, this does not explain why he would be attacked."

"Was Shiva Apte talking to the people that he had hired?" Ramanujan asks, holding on to the seatbelt as his car makes a sharp turn, backing into the driveway. Deputy Inspector Riyad Alam, walking forward to meet him, salutes, as Ramanujan walks out of the car, "were you supposed to go and get the warrant?"

"The judge is emailing it to us, right now." Alam replies, "what did you find at the Chauhan house?"

"Same as always, a great deal of nothing." Inspector Ramanujan walks into his office, Deputy Inspector Alam walking behind him; settling into the chair, he turns around to pick up a paperweight, twirling it over and over in his fingers, "Maan Singh Chauhan actually told me, in no uncertain terms, to leave."

"Leave?"

"Oh, they were forthcoming enough, I believe," the sarcasm in his voice slips forth easily, "to meet any of them, I have to meet with the head of the family first, and only then, will they allow me to meet with the other members. It's infuriating."

"Effective, if you ask me," DI Alam replies, settling down into one of the visitors' chairs, "that way, the entire narrative is controlled by them. None of the family members will talk, until they get permission from the head of the family. It's perfect."

"It's a problem," Ramanujan groans, "are they doing this on purpose? To obstruct the police? What do they hope to achieve from this?"

"Image," Deputy Inspector Alam says, inspecting his fingernails, "they are protecting their image, as most people do. When you have much to lose, all of a sudden, you are prepared to do anything to protect it. There is very little to do with searching for the murderer of their family's trusted steward, or even their own daughter's safety is going to stop them."

"So, Ananya Chauhan might be in danger?" Ramanujan squints, "I thought that the possibility of another attack had been assessed."

"All of that was contingent on the cooperation of the Chauhans," Alam waves a hand, dismissing Ramnujan, a gesture that would have landed him in trouble, if it had been anyone else, "but since the Chauhans are no longer cooperating with us, who is to say that the same people who murdered Shiva Apte will not attack someone of the main family? Ananya Chauhan's wedding is a lavish affair. Anyone could be hiding amidst the crowd."

"That is a far-fetched idea, and you know that too," Ramanujan says, "but we could convince the Chauhans to cooperate, if the protection of their youngest daughter hangs in the balance."

"They are not going to make it easy, by any means." DI Alam says, "at any rate, they are being brought down to the station for questioning tomorrow."

"Good," Ramanujan breathes, putting an arm over his hand, "once this fiasco is over, I'm going to go on a vacation."

"I hear Andaman is perfectly nice this time of the year." Alam replies, "this case willnot be easy to pin down."

After the sub-inspector leaves, Inspector Ramanujan sits up, holding his head in hands. Of course, this case will not be easy. In different circumstances, we have people actually cooperating with us, not a powerful family hell-bent on saving their own skins.

He reaches for the file that the Chauhans had given him, and reaches for the phone.

"Constable Chaudhary," he says into the phone, "do we have a location on Vikram Motwane?"

ଓଃ◈ଃ୦

While Dushyant had, on occasion, visited the police station, in order to converse with Inspector Ramanujan, this was the first time, that he was here, not in order to establish a working relationship with the Inspector, it was to be subjected to questioning, related to the death of one of the most trusted aides of his family. And Shiva had been doing something on the orders of his family, too. In all senses of the word, his family had been the one to murder their trusted steward.

Someone else may have attacked him, but the burden was to be carried by the Chauhan family.

"Dushyant Chauhan," the constable, a rather severe-looking woman says, opening a door, "you may wait inside."

Dushyant complies, entering the room and taking a seat on an uncomfortable chair, observing the room, walls done in a plae white, the edges of the paint peeling off, a large table in the middle of it, around which there are a few scattered chairs. It reminds him of the holding cells from the television shows Ashish likes to watch, where the police officer comes to interrogate the suspect. Am I a suspect now? The lines are blurring, at least for him, the culpability of his own nature too much for him to bear.

We killed him. Our family took a man's life.

"Mr. Chauhan," the door opens, and Inspector Ramanujan enters, followed closely by Deputy Inspector Alam, "I hope you know what you are here for."

"Yes, officer." Dushyant says, not entirely trusting his own voice to say anything beyond the bare minimum.

"Very well, then." The two men take their respective seats, on opposite sides of the table, "this is a simple—questioning. To gather all the facts in order to present a better case. The more you cooperate with us, the better chances we have of apprehending the murderer of Mr Apte."

Dushyant nods. There had been people who were questioned before him, his father, his brothers, and all of them had walked out of the room, single expressions firmly in place, even as he looked at the policemen who escorted him out of the rooms, the furrow in their brows deepening with every member of his family. So, now we are obstructing the course of justice, too. Wonder where this all will end. Do we defraud the government too? Not that we haven't yet already.

"Sure." His reply brings a shared look, between the two officers, "I will try my best."

"That's more than what we have had yet," the deputy inspector murmurs, under his breath, a sentence that Dushyant is not sure if he was supposed to hear. The deputy inspector opens a file, and passes it on to Inspector Ramanujan. The inspector, in turn, pushes it towards Dushyant.

"Do you remember anything about the hiring of extra help for Ananya Chauhan's wedding?"

"Anshul bhaiya was supposed to handle it," Dushyant says weakly, "but Shiva told Anshul bhaiya that he could handle it himself."

"So, you were not involved?" Deputy Inspector Alam's is unconvinced, "it is your daughter's wedding. One would like to think that as her father, you would want to be more involved in these matters."

"We are a joint family," Dushyant grits out, failing to disguise the flash of annoyance that goes through him, "there is no reason for me to oversee such a huge venture by myself. We all had different responsibilities regarding Ananya's wedding."

"And Mr Apte was in charge of overseeing the extra staff?" Inspector Ramanujan asks, "your brother told me that he was also involved in an investment venture, of Lata diamonds."

"Yes." Dushyant responds in a monosyllable, unsure of what else to say. Shiva had been a part of the investment venture, instrumental in bringing in information about Mehra Diamonds. Quite different from Mehra Jewellers, who have been one of their fiercest competitors in the market, this was a smaller company who had only just launched into the market. Dushyant felt a bit apologetic for strong-arming them into accepting a deal that even he knew was not good for them in the long run, but they were the ones who needed the money, not Lata Diamonds. Actually, he didn't even feel bad.

"So, he was involved in the investment venture?"

"Yes, he did research on the company that we invested in, Mehra Diamonds." Dushyant says, "although I was not involved in the deal, I knew most of the details of it."

"From whom?" Ramanujan interrupts him, "I doubt you talk shop at the dinner table, and I do not think Mr Anshul Chauhan is a sweet older brother, who allows you to tag along for the ride."

Dushyant blinks. Once. Twice. Thrice. He breathes, to get his heartbeat under control. I am not a child, he wants to say, I do not tag alongside my brothers. But instead, he says nothing, simply allowing for the moment to pass.

"Is that true, Mr Chauhan?" Ramanujan presses, and Dushyant winces, hoping that it doesn't show on his face, "why were you not involved with the investment dealings?"

Dushyant turns his head, looking away from the two men, "I refused to," he says simply, "I thought that I would only be a nuisance, so I did not attempt to involve myself with the investment dealings. My brothers were already capable enough, so I did not."

"Hmm," Inspector Ramanujan turns to his deputy, and the two of them turn back to Dushyant, "Mr Chauhan, you are the youngest of your brothers, are you not?"

"Yes," Dushyant mutters, "although it is not of any significance. My brothers are far more capable than me, and I do not harbuor any sort of—"

"Are you sure?" the deputy inspector leans back in his seat, "because none of your brothers have been able to help us with this investigation, Mr Chauhan. Then their capability is brought into question, isn't it?"

Dushyant says nothing. Just stares at the table, in lieu of a reply. The surface of the table is wooden, pockmarked, weathered over the years. He wonders, if they have said the same things to his brothers, about the inefficacy of the youngest. You are old enough, damn you. Th voice sounds oddly like his wife. She must be terrified too, being subjected to police questioning like this.

"There is no denying that a man died in your house, Mr Chauhan," Deputy Inspector Alam says, leaning forward again, "that means your family is culpable for it. no matter how you and your brother deny it, no matter how much money Maan Singh Chauhan pays the newspapers and the tabloids, your family will still bear the moral burden of allowing a man to die, in your house. A man who, by all accounts, had been a faithful steward of your estate, fiercely loyal to your company, over the years. You made Shiva Apte do all the dirty work of Lata Diamonds, didn't you? And that is what got him killed."

You made Shiva Apte do all the dirty work, didn't you? And that is what got him killed.

Dushyant had never really been one for the family business, even if he had a mind for it. he much preferred to be overseeing the production aspects of it, instead of the business dealings. They always made him uncomfortable, talking to people, luring them into making bad decisions that would be favourable for the Chauhans, but not for them, all the while pretending to be genuine, all of it, bothered him.

"What did you say?" his father thunders, at the end of the dining table, "my son, to go down to the levels of a mere production engineer? Is that why I paid for your education? Is that what I have raised you to become?"

"No, father," he responds, hanging his head in shame. Why had he expected all of this to go well? With four of his five brothers already in the family business, determined to take Lata Diamonds to greater glory, why would he, as the youngest son of the family, do any different? Anshul, Angad, Abhinav, Ajay, Dushyant. Even his name was different from those of his brothers. "I'm sorry." The apology sounds hollow to his ears, and he knows it, his father too infuriated to notice anything else apart from the infraction that Dushyant has landed on his ego, by refusing to be the son that he wanted him to be.

"Who do you think you are?" his father's words bring him out of his mind, and he focuses again, on the man sitting opposite to him, "how dare you sully the name of the Chauhan family, how dare you refuse my orders!"

Dushyant remains silent. Maan Singh turns to his wife, "Namrata, if I hear this nonsense out of his mouth, once again, I will throw him out of the house!"

Dushyant casts a terrified look at his mother, who simply nods, once, twice. She cannot say anything. Neither can anyone else, for that matter. The only voice that holds any weight, is his father's, and it has been decided.

෯◈ෂ

"Dushyant sahab," Shiva's voice floats out from nowhere, and Dushyant squints to see his family's Old Faithful waiting for him, in the dark, "if Maan Singh Sahab wants you to join the business, there's nothing that you can do to save yourself."

"I know, Shiva, I know," the bitterness spills easily from his tongue, coating it in ashen black, "I know. My father will not stand for anything that goes against his wishes. Anything that I do, therefore, is against his wishes."

"Then you should learn to be more like him."

Dushyant turns to face Shiva so fast he can hear a crick in his neck, "are you insane?"

"Not at all," the other man replies, slight smile on his face, "on the contrary. Let me help you out, Dushyant sahab. I'll help you get settled into the business, and help you with the business dealings. Anything you need help with, I will give it to you."

"And in return?" Dushyant was not stupid. He had a degree from one of the best universities in the country, he was perfectly aware of the ramifications of a favour, "and what do I do for you in return?"

"In return?" Shiva's eyes became distant, "in return, Dushyant sahab, you help me, once. Only once will I ask you for help. But, you have to help me, no questions asked."

And he had failed him.

Dushyant says nothing. Ramanujan can feel the impatience rolling off of the deputy inspector in waves, the tapping on the hard linoleum floor impossible to ignore. He sends Deputy Alam a warning look. The other man simply shrugs, pointing at Dushyant Chauhan, who seems to be caught in a dilemma of his own, seemingly in the midst of an existential crisis. Ramanujan would not like to be in his position.

"Mr Chauhan?" he asks, trying to establish eye contact with the man, "Mr Chauhan, do you have an answer?"

"Yes?" the other man seems to be disoriented for a moment, "yes, could you repeat the question, please?"

We were not asking him a question, Ramanujan muses, God knows where his mind was, right now. "Mr Chauhan," he says, cautious, "what do you remember of the day, when Mr Apte was attacked?"

Dushyant Chauhan looks at him vacantly. "Mr Chauhan," Ramanujan repeats, "what do you remember of the day?"

Focus, Dushyant. He remembers the line that he used to tell himself, back in university, focus, and this too shall pass. All of this, is simply a nightmare. Nothing more, nothing less. Close your eyes, and write whatever you know.

"I was in the west wing of the house when they came to tell me that Shiva had been found," he says, closing his eyes, "I was talking ot Damini—my wife, about the menu that we had decided on, for the wedding. She was talking to me about the mehendi ceremony, to be held in three days. Then, a servant—have I seen him before? I no longer remember, all of it is a blur, came to tell us—sahab, Shiva bhai is lying on the terrace. He's been badly beaten, and there is blood. That is all. I ran, so did Anshul bhaiya—he was there, talking to my father, both of us ran, and found him—Shiva, lying, in the middle of the terrace, blood pooling all around him."

"Hmm," Ramanujan makes a noncommittal noise, "and you called the ambulance then and there?"

"Yes, we did," Dushyant tries to recall, "I called the police, Anshul called the ambulance."

"The police reached before the ambulance, didn't we?" Ramanujan turns to Alam, who nods tersely, "did you call the police before or after your brother called the ambulance?"

"Before," Dushyant says, dazed, "I remember someone telling me to call the police—my brother, Angad. I remember it because Anshul bhaiya had already finished calling the ambulance, and they were all looking at me, wondering, when would I make the call."

"Very well, then," Ramanujan closes the file, "and do you remember where your daughter was?"

"She had gone out with her fiancé, for a drive." Dushyant murmurs, "she did not know anything until I called her home; the second call I made after the police, was to her."

"We found that Mr Apte made a call to your phone before he was attacked. Roughly thirty minutes before he was hit over the head with a blunt object, Mr Shiva Apte made a call to your phone, Mr Chauhan. Could you explain that?"

"I did not receive a call," Dushyant Chauhan looks distressed, "if I had received a call from him, I would have disclosed it to the police. There was no communication between me and him."

DI Alam makes another noncommittal noise, and Inspector Ramanujan proceeds, "I doubt that the phone call went through, given that the reception within your house had been exceptionally bad, for the three days leading up to the attack on Mr Apte, and his subsequent death. Did you think much of it?"

"No, not really," Dushyant confesses, "I did not think much of it, there was too much to be done for Ananya's wedding—my daughter's wedding." The last part of it is a warning, and neither Ramanujan nor Alam mistake it for something else, sharing a look between each other, so, he is cracking, finally. "I had been busy the entire day, with the Mehra investment deal, then the engagement party, then the two weeks that we had, to make it presentable for the guests, most of whom have cancelled their invitations, citing problems that would have never occurred, if someone had not decided t murder my family's steward."

Dushyant takes a deep breath. And continues, "I did not think a lot of the disturbances in network because these are common, at least in our area. And I was not available, for most of the day. I was busy."

"If you were busy conducting your daughter's wedding,' Ramanujan squints, "should you not have been available? You mean to say you went for hours without your phone, and yet, you managed to coordinate such an event flawlessly?"

Dushyant squirms, "I did not say that. I merely—neglected my phone when I was not contacting other people. And the mobile network seems to be having a lot of problem that day, so I did not attend to my phone."

"Very well then, Mr Chauhan," Inspector Ramanujan says, standing up, "you are free to go."

Dushyant looks up, incredulous, "you are letting me go?"

"Yes, you free to leave," Deputy Inspector Alam says, irritated, "we will call you if we have any further questions for you. Till then, you are a free man."

Dushyant stands up, dusting off invisible pieces of lint from his kurta, "thank you, officers."

He only receives a curt nod in reply, before the same sever-faced constable walks in, to escort him away. he could do without the police escort, but a man had died within the safety of his own home. Who knew if they would simply stop, with the death of Shiva? Who was to say, that they would not seek to harm someone of their family? Him, Dushyant Chauhan? His wife? Ananya—no, they would never harm Ananya, Dushyant would make sure of it; he has always protected his only daughter from harm, and would continue to do so, even at the cost of his entire life.

The two of them watch him drive away, in the car that had also brought Ananya Chauhan to the police station. Inspector Ramanujan says nothing, before lighting a cigarette, while Deputy Inspector Alam simply stands there, arms crossed.

"Do you think we should have arrested them?" Deputy Inspector Alam asks, "their actions killed a man, no matter who wielded the weapon in the end. The Chauhans killed an innocent man, and we are to just let them go? Is there no way we can hold them? For something other than aiding and abetting murder?"

"No, Alam," Inspector Ramanujan says, the white smoke of the cigarette curling around his hand, before disappearing into the air, "we cannot arrest them, neither can we hold them and question them further, on the basis of our suspicions. There is too much riding on this case. It's giving me a headache."

"Me too."

Ramanujan's phone pings with a notification. He unlocks the device, reads it, before smiling, "let's go, Alam. We need to pay a visit to the Chauhan family mansion. The judge finally signed the search warrant."

"Yes sir."

Chapter 4

AN INTERROGATION

"But how could you live, and have no story to tell?"

– Fyodor Dostoevsky

"A search warrant?" Judge Dubey asks, seated in his office, "which case are you talking about?"

"The Chauhan case, sir," Inspector Ramanujan slides the file towards Judge Dubey, "we believe that the Chauhans may be hiding documents of importance."

"And you want to search their offices and home?" Judge Dubey responds, "well, didn't you already seize all the possessions of the deceased?"

"We did sir, but—" Inspector Ramanujan pauses for a moment, before continuing, "—I don't think they complied with everything. Neither do I think they will, if we ask them to cooperate politely."

"You're worried about obstruction of justice?"

"I'm worried about evidence being erased," Inspector Ramanujan replies, "if we don't have the warrant, then we become dependent on their willingness to share information with us, which is already too low."

"Don't insinuate, Inspector," Judge Dubey laughs, "I might have you be sued for slander."

Inspector Ramanujan frowns, "Sir, we do require this warrant, and we need it as soon as possible. There is not much time in our hands."

Judge Dubey looks at the man, and then sighs, before picking up his pen to sign the search warrant. "Be careful, inspector," he says, as Ramanujan makes his way to leave the office, "you seem to be treating the Chauhans like the suspects, too."

"I'm a policeman, your honour," Inspector Ramanujan calls out, turning around for a brief moment, "it's my job to be suspicious."

ೞ◈ಬ

Delhi roads were not always smooth, but Deputy Inspector Alam found this ride, along bumpy asphalt, to be the most pleasant one of his life. It was not that he had some sort of vendetta against the Chauhans, neither did he have any particular hatred for them.

Deputy Inspector Alam simply hated liars.

And oh, they had been lying outright. From the old patriarch, Maan Singh, who refused to even talk to him, and Anshul Chauhan, who regarded him with a sort of cruel unfamiliarity and arrogance, cultivated by years of entitlement, owing to his status, money, power. None of them spoke the truth, or even attempted at speaking the truth, repeating the same three excuses, over and over again. All of them, except for Dushyant Chauhan, the youngest son.

"Sir, we are almost there," the driver says, and Deputy Inspector Alam peers out of the car, at the giant and imposing mansion, rising up in a manner eerily similar to that of a gothic castle, full of secrets, whispering to each other in the dark.

He supposes that the people who live here, have never faced a single day of misfortune. Maybe this is their first brush with death. First brush that we know of. Who knows what has happened before.

The gates open up before the car, and he straightens himself. Would not do to have them think of me as a fool.

Inspector Ramanujan walks in front of him, up to the large wooden doors, and Alam takes a look at the compound around them. of course, there is a wedding ongoing. Flowers, half-scattered, a gazebo, propped up and in the process of being decorated. There was still some time for Ananya Chauhan's wedding, but it looked like either the people had stopped mid-way, or they were all waiting, for something to happen. He suspects that a sight of three police vans, with policemen in both plain and uniform dress, has made the people in the neighbourhood start to talk, no matter how secluded it might be.

The doors open, and it's not any of the numerous servants that open it, but Damini Chauhan, Dushyant Chauhan's wife.

"I thought we were all done being questioned." She says, by way of greeting. Alam can feel the constables bristle underneath the scrutiny of her sharp gaze, and says nothing. Inspector Ramanujan stands at the front of their group.

"Search warrant, Mrs Chauhan," his superior says, with no smile on his face, "we are here to search your home."

"And if I refuse to allow you in?"

"Then you shall be charged with obstruction of justice," he says, easy, "excuse us."

And then, they begin.

⚜

Inspector Ramanujan has never liked Aditya Mehra. Given the fact that he had met with the youngest boy of the Mehra family on more than one occasion, he thought that he had a pretty good idea of who the boy was. The typical rich of Delhi, the people who got away with everything just because of their family's money, power and prestige—leaving someone else to take the fall for their own actions.

His distaste for people like them grows bigger, if possible.

"Sir," Deputy Inspector Alam enters his office, "he's in the interrogation room. Should I go in with you?"

"No, don't worry about that," Ramanujan replies, "I don't want the tabloids saying that the police mistreated their youngest son."

"He is a suspect, sir."

"And we are still bound, hand and foot, with the privilege and power these people have," Ramanujan wonders for a moment why his own word sound so much like his deputy's full of ideals and determination, "we need to keep him here for the foreseeable future, while simultaneously arresting the people he had most likely hired for murdering Shiva Apte. It was a shame that they couldn't finish the job."

"Well," Deputy Inspector Alam snickers, "about a hundred people bought drugs off of him last night, including one of our own undercover officers. We have had our eyes on him for a long time."

"We'll ask for Narcotics' help on this later, after the Chauhan case has made some sort of headway. Any lead on the computers and ledgers we found at the residence?"

"None so far, sir, but we are working on Mr Apte's personal computer. Perhaps he has something there that might prove his case."

"He has. You just need to find it. I have met Shiva Apte," Ramanujan leans back in the chair, picking up a glass paperweight, "he was a very smart man. If he had been doing the Chauhan family's dirty work, at least something that would get him killed, or at the very least, in danger, he would have insurance. Some kind of proof of what he had been doing, that it had been ordered by the Chauhans themselves."

"I thought Shiva Apte was loyal to the Chauhans," his deputy seems a bit unsettled by this information, "sir, are you sure that is the case? Shiva Apte was the loyal employee of the Chauhan family for many years, I doubt he would have dirt on his own employers."

"He wasn't a loyal employee, he was a loyal dog," Ramanujan says evenly, "he was the Chauhan family's dog, and even dogs have self-respect. There is a limit to one's unquestioned loyalty. I have found that death, even the threat of it, is one of them."

Inspector Ramanujan stands up, straightening his shirt collar, "let's go pay Aditya Mehra a visit, Deputy Inspector."

Aditya Mehra sits at the table, feet atop the wood surface. His face is twisted in an elegant, handsome smile. No doubt working out the ways of getting his father's power and his own societal privilege ot walk out of here, scot-free. He had been charged before, once, twice. But that had been under different circumstances, not that of a possible conspiracy to murder charge. Ramanujan sighs, before pushing the door open, walking inside.

"Mr Mehra." It's a short enough introduction, enough to pull the attention of the man to him, and Ramanujan settles himself down into a chair, "my deputy is not with me today, so feel free to make yourself comfortable."

"Alam?" the young man raises an eyebrow, "good for him, I would say. It always helps to know one's own place."

Of course. He never did well with respect. "The same sentiment applies to you too, Mr Mehra," Ramanujan smiles at the man, taking only a little bit of joy at the way his face falls at the sentence, and the implication, "you were caught selling drugs to people at Divine, a club in South Delhi, last night. You attempted to sell cocaine to a policeman in plain dress, amongst tens of other people. You do realise, that if this gets out, your father will not be able to save you?"

Aditya Mehra smiles, his upper lip curling in on itself, "you do realise that I will still find myself out of here before the day ends? And then, when the public finds out what you have done to the son of the Mehra family, what will happen then?"

"Whatever happens, happens." Ramanujan gives Aditya a serene smile, "you don't have to be so worried about me."

"Ah, of course I'm not. And I expect that my father's close friendship with both the commissioner and the Chief Minister is nothing to worry about, for you."

A muscle begins to tick, in the corner of Ramanujan's forehead. Aditya Mehra liked to threaten people, apparently, even when he was driven to a corner. "I can assure you, that will not be a problem."

"You, on the other hand—I'm sorry, but having the son of a high-profile businessman sell drugs at a Delhi club is just the sort of things that tabloids like to pick up on. Notwithstanding the years you will get in prison for possession and distribution of drugs."

"A son."

"What?"

"My father has three sons. I'm only one of them, and the youngest, to boot. I am not the only son of my father." Aditya Mehra says, tone clipped.

"Very well, a son of a high-profile businessman," Ramanujan concedes, "you were caught on camera, selling to a police officer."

"Then there's nothing to it, is there?" the man leans back in his chair, "I suppose I must go to prison for all my sins. Even though the officer in plain clothes approached me first, I am the one who has to take the blame."

"You were selling cocaine to him."

"And I don't sell to people I do not know," Mehra's tone was becoming increasingly flippant, tripping over words and exaggerated hand gestures. Good. Let me see where I have you. "If I did not know this officer of yours, then I would not have sold to him."

"But you did. The officer had been introduced to you by an informant of ours, something you failed to see, Mr Mehra." Ramanujan mimics the man, leaning back, relishing the way his eyes widen at this piece of news. "Bit of an oversight, that. Thought you would have more experience."

Aditya Mehra does not say anything, simply looks at the wood surface of the table. Inspector Ramanujan suddenly remembers Dushyant Chauhan, who had been sitting in the same place, only a few days ago. Both of them were similar, in some aspects; younger sons of families that did not bother to care about them, working to prove themselves to the family. All efforts being futile, of course. Maan Singh regards Dushyant as nothing but a mere placeholder, and he's sure that the Mehra family's patriarch, Ravinder Mehra, also regards Aditya as nothing more. Simply a placeholder for all his older brothers, highly expendable.

"You do realise," he begins his next sentence by choosing his words very carefully, "that you are not going to get out of this situation. There are witnesses that have seen you both possess and distribute drugs. You are going to be fined, sent to prison. Worse, if the judge decides to make an example out of you."

"An example?" Aditya Mehra is now leaning forward, his cuffed hands set on the table. He was keeping it out of sight before. Now, well, he is not so sure, is he?

"Half the city already thinks the worst of your kind—spoilt rich brats who have nothing to their names except for their father's power and prestige. The newspapers spend yards of newsprint on telling the public exactly how one of you brats managed to drive drunk and run over a street-dweller's legs—oh right, that was you."

Aditya bristles, clearly affected, and Ramanujan continues, "but, my proposition might help."

"Help? Are you seriously suggesting I become an informant?" Aditya Mehra looks at him, with all the distaste that he can gather in his current state, "I don't think so. No way."

"Even if there were people in the party last night, people you want to protect by going to prison in their stead, what makes you think that we would not catch them?" He had always been rather good at interrogation. Getting the right information out of people when they were being particularly reticent was a favourite pastime of his, "in this situation, you stand to benefit, if you look at it this way."

"There is nothing that I can say, that might help you," Mehra says, resolute, despite the imminent danger. Ramanujan decides that he probably has no idea how hard prison life can be, only thinking of it as a temporary stop that he must go through. A rite of passage, as one may call, "I already know nothing. The drugs? Sure, that was me, I did it, I'll confess, I'll pay the fines and go to prison. But there's nothing more to that, more than I can tell you."

"Very well, Mr Mehra," Ramanujan stands up, "you will be produced in front of a magistrate this afternoon. Make sure to call your attorney beforehand. If you cannot afford an attorney, one will be provided to you by the state."

Chapter 5

DRUGS

"You never really understand a person until you consider things from his point of view... Until you climb inside of his skin and walk around in it."

– Harper Lee

"Is this a bail hearing?" Aditya Mehra asks Inspector Ramanujan, being escorted to the dock, "why would anyone even pay for my bail?"

"All charges related to narcotics are non-bailable, Mr Mehra," Inspector Ramanujan replies, "you're being produced in front of the magistrate, to extend your police custody."

"So, even if I say the truth about the drugs, you're going to put me here?" Aditya Mehra does not sound surprised, nor does he sound affronted, only resigned, quiet, "of course, I did expect this. There is always risk as well as reward involved in these matters."

"Risk and reward?" Inspector Ramanujan scoffs, "risk and reward doesn't mean dealing in drugs now, does it?"

"It doesn't mean being born as me, either?" Aditya Mehra argues, "either way, I was the one who was caught dealing drugs."

"Or, you could just tell us the nmes of the people that you are trying to protect." Inspector Ramanujan says, as three court guards take away aditya Mehra by the cuffs, "they aren't going to come and help you, so what is the point?"

ଓ◈ୠ

"Sir," "Deputy Inspector Alam announces himself, entering the room, "we managed to get a hold of Aditya Mehra's cousin, Vikram. On his mother's side, so we didn't think too much of him on the first background check done on Aditya Mehra."

"Skip the formalities, Alam," Ramanujan says, "what is the evidence?"

"His bank account had about twenty-five lakhs transferred to it, right after the news of shiva Apte's death was announced." Here, Alam pauses, checking a file, "I suspect that the money was wired from an offshore company, but we cannot be sure until the bank statements come through. I'll interrogate him, if you want."

"He wasn't paid until the news of Shiva Apte's death was broadcast, right?" Ramanujan stands up, abrupt, "when was the transaction made?"

"At three-fifteen in the morning, sir." Alam hands him the file, containing the bank records of Vikram, the cousin of Aditya Mehra, "twenty-five lakhs, wow. That's a lot of money."

"They give out bribes larger than this on a Tuesday afternoon, Alam," Ramanujan chides, "focus. The fact that the money was deposited into his account minutes after Shiva Apte's death means one of two things—that wither the news was leaked to members of the press, and they simply did not publish it until the next morning, but there was no mention of it in any of the websites. Otherwise, well, there is simply one more explanation there, although I doubt people would take it very well."

Deputy Inspector Alam's face is inscrutable, as he sinks onto a chair, "sir, are you implying that one of the Chauhan family members might have had Mr Apte murdered? But why?"

"Same reason that I believe there is something incriminating on Shiva Apte's computer, Alam," Inspector Ramanujan says, "loyalty is not absolute. Never has been, never will be. The Chauhans have something to do with this case, as do the Mehras."

Deputy Inspector Alam does not say anything, checking his phones for an update, "sir, they finished working on both Shiva Apte's laptop and the bank account from where the money was transferred to Vikram's bank account. They need you to be there."

"Very well," Inspector Ramanujan stands up, "let's go and find out what exactly this is about."

ଓ◈ଥ

Indrani Chaudhari was a woman of few words. Highly efficient, almost scary in the way she executed things. Deputy Inspector Alam has always been slightly wary of her, lest he say something to infuriate the woman and be on the receiving end of the worst dressing-down he would ever hear in his life. He's already seen it happen once.

"Officer Chaudhari," Ramanujan says, pleasantly, walking into her office, "I hear you have the reports ready."

"Sure," the woman replies, pushing the file over the tabletop, "the bank account that gave the money was an offshore one, set up to launder money for the Mehras, most likely. If we look further, we can find a link to the Mehras, or specifically, Aditya Mehra."

Deputy Inspector Alam nods, "I assume there's more to it than meets the eye, is it?"

"The money in the offshore account was not there when Shiva Apte died."

"What do you mean?"

"I mean that twenty-five lakhs had been wired to the offshore bank account, just after Shiva Apte's death," Officer Chaudhari highlights a line in the document, "this line. The money came from an affiliate company of Lata Diamonds. The Chauhans' investment firm, to be precise. They wired it through the account of a minor employee, who was then promptly fired. Probably forced them to do it. In any case, no matter how you look at it, the whole thing was orchestrated on multiple levels—both by the Mehras and the Chauhans."

"The Mehras and the Chauhans have been at loggerheads for the better part of a decade," Inspector Ramanujan says, smile playing on his lips, "they would not be coming together to remove one single obstacle, shared as it may be."

"Aditya Mehra fell out of favour with his father." Deputy Inspector Alam says, looking at the two of them, "what? Did neither of you read the tabloids this morning?"

"No, we did not," Ramanujan says, "go on, then."

"The head of the Mehra family, Ravinder Mehra said that he, 'did not consider' his youngest son to be a part of the family any more." Alam finishes, putting air quotes around 'did not consider'. "My opinion is that Aditya Mehra's fallout with his father had already happened, just that the newspapers did not get wind of it."

"Even so, you cannot prosecute someone from the Chauhan family based on a hunch."

"You can, however, prosecute Aditya Mehra. He is the liability here, not his cousin and the hired thugs that murdered Shiva Apte."

"Speaking of Shiva Apte," Indrani Chaudhari cuts in, "his laptop had a lot of information, most of it deleted a few hours before his death. A lot of records of the Lata Diamonds business. Even more of the family's records."

"Figures," Ramanujan says, thoughtful, "he was the family's longtime employee."

"That would have made sense if he had been using the information for the use of the Chauhans," Officer Chaudhari waves a hand, dismissing it, "he used it for an entirely different purpose."

"What do you mean?"

"Shiva Apte had been exchanging emails with a protected account. Most of it was run-of-the-mill, names of people in the hierarchy, the executives of the diamond business. Some of it dealt with more in-depth details, such as stock market information."

"Corporate espionage?" Deputy Inspector Alam doesn't believe a word of what she's saying, "so he got killed over corporate espionage?"

"Maybe," Officer Chaudhari shrugs, "in the last email, however, he does not write about the company."

"What does he write about, then?" Inspector Ramanujan takes the proffered file, "I have the information you requested, about Hisar. What does Hisar have to do with this?"

"Looks like he was digging up information on something that happened some time before." Deputy Inspector Alam says, looking over Ramanujan's shoulder, "it would make sense. While both the Mehra and the Chauhan families are from Hisar, neither of them have stepped foot in Haryana since 1990."

"Thirty years is a long time," Officer Chaudhari says, "why do you think they moved to Delhi?"

"Something must have happened in Hisar that the Chauhans are not telling us," Inspector Ramanujan stands up, "thank you, Officer Chaudhari. You were of immense help."

∞◈∞

Aditya Mehra looks like a shell of himself.

That is the first thought that goes through Deputy Inspector Alam's mind, peering at the younger man sitting in one of the station jail cells. The court had ordered him ten days in police custody, and from the looks of it, he was not taking to it very well. When they had brough him into the station, Mehra looked like he had stepped off of a page three article, arrogance seeping out of him, self-assured in his freedom. Now, seven days later, he looked gaunt, his clothes now dirt-streaked from the floor of the holding cells. How the mighty have fallen. Alam would have taken some pity on him, if he did not know Aditya Mehra to be one of the worst people, he had ever had the misfortune of encountering.

"Are you not going to interrogate him for the Chauhan case?" he asks, walking into Inspector Ramanujan's office, "it has been a week already. We have solid leads connecting him to the case."

"Did you know Ananya Chauhan got married?"

Deputy Inspector Alam massages his temples, albeit discreetly. Inspector Ramanujan was being distracted again. Who cares if Ananya Chauhan got married? Did she order the Mehra boy to hire people to murder Shiva Apte? If no, then she can marry the Chief Minister for all I care, "no, sir," he says, settling himself into a seat, "I did not know Miss Chauhan got married. I suppose congratulations are in order."

"Yes, I suppose so, Alam," the Inspector replies, "ah, it's Mrs Rathi now."

"What?"

Inspector Ramanujan turns the monitor, and Deputy Inspector Alam peers at the screen. The youngest daughter of the Chauhan Family marries Sooraj Rathi, owner of Rathi Consulting firm in a private ceremony at the Chauhan family residence in Delhi. "Her fiancé—husband's name is Rathi?"

"Yes, Alam," Ramanujan leans back into his chair, "Ananya Chauhan is now Ananya Rathi."

"Forgive me for asking this sir," Alam feels slightly impudent, saying this to his superior, "but is it really relevant to our investigation?"

"Perhaps, perhaps not," Ramanujan sits up again, "somehow, I have a feeling it is. Extremely important. There seems to be something that I have missed."

"The interrogation. For the Chauhan case. Aditya Mehra." Deputy Inspector Alam responds, deadpan. If I do not drag him onto the right track, he will get lost in his thoughts, again. Three days later, we need to provide the formal charges for indictment. If we don't ger Aditya Mehra to spill the beans, he will be released on bail, or sent to prison. Either way, we lose a witness, and perhaps the only lead in this investigation.

"Ah, yes, the Mehra boy." Inspector Ramanujan snaps his fingers, "right, let's go, Alam."

೮◈ಐ

"Mr Mehra," Inspector Ramanujan announces himself before entering, thick folder in hand, "sorry to disturb you again. This is my colleague, Deputy Inspector Alam."

Aditya Mehra says nothing, simply glares at the two of them, half a challenge in his eyes. Despite being handcuffed, Alam finds himself reconsidering his earlier opinion of Aditya Mehra on the holding cells.

"I still have three days until I have to be produced before the court again," Aditya Mehra says, boredly. "I doubt both of you are here to see me about drugs."

"You selling drugs in the middle of a Delhi club is still a hot topic," Deputy Inspector Alam snipes, "even if you manage to secure bail in the court, you are going to be vilified by the papers for—"

"—about a week," Aditya Mehra interrupts, glare levelled at Alam, "the newspapers will hold the story for about a week. Then, something else will crop up, something far mor interesting. A politician's son, captured visiting a brothel. A minister, brought in on charges of corruption. There are more things to capture the interest of the public than the philandering and wayward son of a businessman, as high-profile as he may be. Then what will you do? Put me on trial again? I cannot be prosecuted for the same crime twice."

"I was sure Deputy Inspector Alam would know better than to argue with me," Aditya Mehra continues, "but I suspect he still does not know his place."

"Are you sure?" Inspector Ramanujan takes his seat, "because I'm sure the involvement of a high-profile businessman's son, in an ongoing murder investigation, would not only capture the public's interest, but also hold it, for a very long time."

Aditya Mehra's face falls, his eyes widening. Only for a split second, however, before he schools it back into the perfectly arrogant mask, no doubt practiced and perfected over many, many years, "I do not know what you are talking about."

"Of course, you don't," Ramanujan says, pleasantly, "take a look at that. It's the account statement for your cousin, Vikram. He's already confessed to everything."

No one says anything. Deputy Inspector Alam's eyes are trained on Aditya Mehra's face, looking for anything that might give him away. Aditya Mehra and Ramanujan, in turn, are staring at each other, gauging each other for a reaction.

Finally, after what seems like an eternity (thirty seconds), Aditya Mehra is the first to speak, "that is—news. I do not know anything about Vikram anymore."

"Is that why you wired twenty-five lakhs from an offshore bank account to his? Because you do not know anything about him?" Inspector Ramanujan takes a pen, underlining the credit statement, "there. The account is in your name. probably your father set it up, in order to ease the pain of laundering money. Then, when you came of age, he turned over the account to you. In any case, even if the account was discovered, Ravinder Mehra could always say that you were the one embezzling from the company, and he would get off scot-free."

Aditya Mehra snorts. "You have no idea about my father, then, if you think he's going to be so straightforward with everything," he drawls, "if he did that, everyone would know what he was doing. He would not do that. Too easy."

"Then what would he do?"

Aditya Mehra seems to weigh his options for a moment, then shrugs, "not telling. If I tell you, then that's just the easy way out."

"Then I suppose you will have to tell us why the twenty-five lakhs were wired to your account first, and then from you, to Vikram's account?" Inspector Ramanujan smiles, "we can be here all day, Mr Mehra, if that is what you want us to do. But twenty-five lakhs were wired to your account, at three-fifteen in the morning, approximately ten minutes after Shiva Apte's death."

Aditya Mehra's lips curl, "ooh, you are good. Never thought I would be saying that about Delhi Police."

Deputy Inspector Alam forces down the flash of irritation in his stomach. Let him speak, Inspector Ramanujan had said, before stepping foot into the room, let him incriminate himself. He's much more use to us as a witness than as a prisoner.

"Do you know what I think, Mr Mehra?" Inspector Ramanujan says, standing up, "I think that the person who sent you the money, is someone that you work for. Simply put, you are the middleman here. Neither the executioner, nor the plotter. A middleman, only trying to do his job. If you give us information, instead of protecting whoever it is that you are protecting," Ramanujan starts pacing, "the government will make sure that you are safe."

Aditya Mehra laughs, a hollow, low sound, that rings off the walls of the room. Deputy Inspector Alam grips his pen, hard.

"Well, what do you want to know?"

Chapter 6

THE FIRST HEARING

"There is something rotten in the state of Denmark."

– William Shakespeare

"All rise."

Dushyant Chauhan had never really been inside a courtroom. Of course, the company has had cases against them, petty ones, but they had all been handled by their lawyers. Never had he been in the middle of a courtroom, waiting to see the proceedings of a trial.

Aditya Mehra, charged with conspiracy to murder. There were more charges too, but Dushyant did not bother to remember all of them, instead allowing the information to slip out of his mind as soon as it had been learnt of. We have nothing to do with the Mehras. This will not come back to us. He cannot deny the relief that comes with this knowledge, that the murder of their most loyal servant, was not because of their family, but because of someone else, someone who was a stranger to them.

Aditya Mehra was a few years older than Ananya, about the same age as Ashish. Dushyant sighs. If only he had not—well, there was nothing much they could do about it anymore.

None of the Chauhans were present this afternoon—only Dushyant, sitting by himself as the proceedings unfold in front of him. he had asked his father to make an appearance, but as usual, Maan Sing Chauhan was less than interested in legal proceedings.

Even for someone who had served us so loyally over the past years? Dushyant had lost track of the time that Shiva had been working for them. it always seemed as though he was a part of their family, someone who would always be there, alongside him, his brothers, his father, everyone. And now, the man who had worked so tirelessly for the Chauhan family was dead, with no one to even attend the court proceedings.

"It's a waste of time," his brother, Angad, had said, as Dushyant was stepping out of the house, "you know, nothing much will happen today. They are not going to sentence him to prison this afternoon. Going there would be a waste of time."

"Angad bhaiya." Dushyant's own tone was a warning, and not a warning, stepping away before it became ugly between them, as he has always done, "should we not go to the court proceedings then?"

"Go when the verdict is going to be given, not on a day when the court merely decides to put the Mehra boy in custody." Angad poured himself a glass of water, "I assume you are taking the day off?"

"No." Dushyant had said, lying as easily as he breathed, "I'll spend no more than an hour in there."

"See that you do not." Angad's words had been a warning, "I will not be dealing with you if you miss any of the meetings today. It'll be Anshul bhaiya."

Dushyant nodded tightly, walking out of the house. Of course, Anshul, his eldest brother, would be the one to enforce the will of his father.

Aditya Mehra was sentenced to thirteen days in court custody, before he was sentenced to be produced in front of the court again. So much for anything happening this afternoon, Dushyant thinks, picking up his briefcase and making a hasty exit through to the court lawn, checking his watch. Two hours before the scheduled meeting with the jewellery workers. Plenty of time.

"Mr Chauhan!"

The words are uttered by Inspector Ramanujan, who was now walking towards him at a brisk pace, with the deputy inspector behind him. Dushyant stiffens. He has not forgotten the interrogation yet.

"Ah yes, Inspector Ramanujan," he says, nodding his head, "good afternoon."

"Here to see the proceedings?" Inspector Ramanujan asks, "well, nothing much will happen today, I hope you know that."

"Yes, I know," Dushyant says, "still, thought I could attend the proceedings."

Inspector Ramanujan merely raises an eyebrow, and behind him, the Deputy inspector merely glowers. Still, Dushyant does not acknowledge the guilt that propelled him to attend, putting it away, to be dealt with later.

"We will need to interrogate you again, Mr Chauhan," Inspector Ramanujan says, "I do hope that you will comply with the orders given."

"And if I do not?"

"Then we shall simply be forced to produce an arrest warrant." Inspector Ramanujan turns on his heel, walking back to the courtroom. Dushyant only stares.

So, if I don't comply, they bring an arrest warrant. But if I do, then I go against my family. Either way, I am the sole villain of this narrative.

ೞ◈ಐ

Ananya was in the kitchen, cooking breakfast for Sooraj. Her husband. *My husband,* she thinks happily, placing perfectly cooked slices of toast on the plate, *I am now Mrs Ananya Rathi.*

Her father had called her the previous night, asking her about the court hearing the previous day. Ananya had said nothing, not willing to go to the courthouse to observe the trial. *Nothing would happen today anyway.* She had said that she was busy, even though her father had not really asked her to accompany him. *of course, he never did.* Her father never really asked her to do these things. Not that Ananya herself wanted to go, sitting in on the courtroom proceedings, where the person who ordered the death of her Shiva uncle. She would never go there, to look at the man who ordered her oldest confidante to be murdered in cold blood.

From her childhood, she remembered Shiva *bhaiya,* always present in their home, in their lives, with a smileo n his face. So many summer afternoons spent playing hide-and-seek in the large gardens of her home. All the years that she had spent in her house, with Shiva *bhai* as a fixed part of her household, gone in an instant. All of it seems like a nightmare, one that she cannot wake from.

"Ananya?" Sooraj enters the kitchen, holding up two ties in either hand, "should I go with a pattern, or a solid tie?"

Ananya shakes her head violently, before turning to focus on a smiling Sooraj, who was still holding the two pieces of fabric aloft, "I think the solid-coloured one works better," she says, smiling, "it suits the pattern on your suit jacket better."

"Really?" Sooraj smiles, and Ananya turns away to focus on her cooking, still smiling, "I heard your father was calling you last night?"

Ananya turns, straining the tea, "he asked me if I wanted to go and see the court proceedings of Shiva *bhaiya's* case. The murder trial started this morning, and I think *papa* went to see it." She tuns to Sooraj, tapping her chin thoughtfully, "How did you know?"

Sooraj laughs, "you did talk a bit loudly last night, Ananya." There is no reproach in his voice, but Ananya feels guilty, nevertheless, "sorry I did not ttell you beforehand."

"You did tell me now," Sooraj takes a seat, "I am sorry too. I was simply a bit confused, after overhearing the conversation last night."

"It was a bit confusing," Ananya laughs, before walking to the table, "I didn't even realise that the trial was today."

"It's simply an initial hearing," Sooraj reasons, "besides, the man responsible—Aditya Mehra—apparently, he confessed to everything himself. Open-and-shut case, and won't take too much time in the courts either."

Ananya frowns. "I hope so. I don't want this to drag on any further than what it has to. Already there has been a lot of talk about Lata Diamonds, and not all of it good. The share prices have fallen too."

"Did *papa* tell you all this?" Sooraj asks, slightly confuses, "but I thought that he never really talked to you about the business."

"He did not," Ananya clarifies, "my mother told me, just after I moved here. She said that the share prices were falling for a while, and that they had stabilised only after our wedding."

Sooraj simply nods, instead of responding to her statement, and Ananya does not say anything further. Sure, the stock of both their companies had risen after their marriage, but Sooraj never really liked to be reminded of that fact. The knowledge that even their wedding, as shrouded in grief as it had been, was used by their families and their companies as a tool for bolstering their own reputations, never sat down well with Sooraj. Ananya herself was used to it, but Sooraj was not, and he never really wanted to fit in, either.

It was not as though their wedding had been one of great pomp. Ananya herself had cancelled half the festivities, and the wedding was simple, a shadow of grief hanging over the whole house as they finished the rituals. Ananya missed Shiva *bhaiya*, the person that she knew would be the happiest on her wedding day.

Her phone rings. Inspector Ramanujan. "Hello?"

"Mrs Rathi," the voice of Inspector Ramanujan over the phone was much more stern, more authoritative than she had remembered, "we would like to talk to you about some details of the case of Mr Shiva Apte."

Ananya feels a chill go down her spine. *So, this is about Shiva bhaiya again. God, who would do this?*

"Do—do I need to be there soon?" she asks, voice breaking, "I'm sorry, it's just that—"

"As soon as possible, Mrs Rathi," the voice of Inspector Ramanujan becomes harsher, "if you do not comply, then the law forces me to produce an arrest warrant for you, Mrs Rathi."

"I will be there as soon as possible," she says, hanging up the phone, "Sooraj, I'm leaving!"

"Wait, Ananya—" Sooraj calls out after her, but Ananya was already out of the house.

Chapter 7

ANANYA

"We spoil ourselves with scrupules, as long
as things go well."

– Aeschylus

"The court calls Mrs Ananya Rathi to the stand."

Ananya stands up, walking rather stiffly to the stand. A witness for the prosecution. *Very well.*

"Mrs Rathi," Prosecutor Deshpande asks, "were you ever acquainted with the accused, Mr Aditya Mehra?"

"Aditya Mehra?" Ananya's brow furrows, "he was a childhood friend of mine. We moved in the same circles. It was impossible to not know Aditya Mehra. However, I was not close with him."

"Yes, of course," The prosecutor smiles, an action that was supposed to put her at ease, but which only served to increase her nerves, "I suppose it would be difficult to ne civil to each other."

"We were civil," Ananya grits out, "I was thinking of inviting him to the wedding, too. But my parents were against the idea of having the Mehras step foot into our home again."

"So, you refused to invite Mr Mehra. What happened on the day of the incident? After you came down from the terrace, having finished your bridal fitting, what happened then?"

Ananya pauses, taking a moment at the newer direction of questioning. "I went for a drive with Sooraj. Shiva *bhaiya* went up to the terrace to call me."

"In your statement to the police, you have mentioned that Shiva Apte preferred to avoid the terrace of the house, and yet he was there on the terrace, the day that he was murdered." The prosecutor says, "forgive me, Mrs Rathi, but I find this coincidence a little bit hard to believe."

"I'm saying the truth!" Ananya almost shouts, hands curling into fists, "he used to avoid the terrace, yes, but I don't know why he went up on the terrace that day! I was away, for hours, when he was attacked!"

"According to the police statements," Prosecutor Deshpande holds up a piece of paper, "you were the last person to see Shiva Apte alive, were you not?"

"I was."

"And what did you notice about him?"

"He was the same as usual," Ananya replies, "he was excited about the wedding. All of us were."

"No more questions, my lord." Prosecutor lawyer stands up.

"Mrs Rathi," he says, without much of a preface, "did you kill Shiva Apte?"

"What are you talking about?" now, Ananya does shout, "why would I kill Shiva Apte?"

"You were getting married in a few days," the lawyer shrugs, "perhaps he had stumbled upon some sort of a secret of yours, a secret that you were willing to kill over."

"Even if I had such a secret," Ananya replies, "I would not murder the person who had raised me. Shiva *bhaiya* was my closest friend. Why would I kill someone I love? and why would I frame Aditya Mehra for it?"

"Because you wished to marry Aditya Mehra."

"Objection, my lord, the defence is purely speculating now." Prosecutor Deshpande stands up, "I don't see why this information is necessary, even if it is true, which it is not."

"Sustained." The Judge replies, "no speculation in a court of law, please."

"Apologies, my lord," the defence lawyer says quickly, before looking back to Ananya, "were you supposed to get married to Aditya Mehra?"

Ananya blanches. *What—how did they know this?* "I—yes. When we were ten, we did plan on getting married. But we never really followed through, and our families never mixed in the same circles, so our childhood fantasies remained the same, fantasies. I have had no contact with him in recent years."

"Even when he moved in the same social circles?" The defence lawyer says, "you were in contact with him because of the position your families enjoyed in society, weren't you?"

"No, I wasn't." Ananya says, "what are you even talking about?"

"So, you were never jealous of him? never despised him? Never found him attractive?"

"What nonsense are you talking about?" Ananya bristles, "does it matter if we were friends or not? If he had Shiva *Bhaiya* killed, then he should pay the price!"

"I think, Mrs Rathi," the defence lawyer steps closer to her, "I think you wished to get married to Aditya Mehra, and when he rejected you, you planned to bring him down. Which is why you had Shiva Apte killed, which is why you had Aditya Mehra framed."

"Stop saying nonsense!" Ananya says, "where would I even get the money to make someone murder for me? what are you talking about?"

The defence lawyer shrugs, stepping back, "no more questions," he says, "thank you my lord."

Ananya leans over the banister, head in hands.

⚬◈⚬

"Mrs Rathi."

Inspector Ramanujan said nothing as Ananya slid into the seat in front of him, the answer was instead, supplied by Deputy Inspector Alam. The girl gives him a grateful smiles, settling down into the seat, "I'm sorry for being so late," Ananya supplied, smiling tightly, "I came as soon as I could."

"Yes, of course," Deputy Inspector Alam says, and the sarcasm in his voice is not lost on Inspector Ramanujan. However, Ananya does not catch on to it, and even if she does, shows no indication of knowing the details of the tone of Deputy Inspector Alam's words, and does not seem to mind. Instead, she offers the other man a grateful smiles, and Inspector Ramanujan sees his subordinate avert his eyes, "we do have a few question to ask you."

Inspector Ramanujan does not say anything other than nodding along to the words of his junior. Ananya Rathi settles into the chair, and looks at the two of them.

"Go ahead, Inspector," she says, "I will answer to the best of my abilities."

"We did ask you questions already," Inspector Ramanujan says, "but these are a bit different."

"Did you notice anything strange with your father, or your Shiva *bhaiya* on the day of the incident" Deputy Inspector Alam asks, "your wedding was in a fortnight, and it was the day of your engagement rituals."

"What do you mean by *anything strange?*"

The girl asks the two of them, and Inspector Ramanujan makes his way to Ananya Rathi, sitting opposite her at the table, "Ananya," he begins, tone soft, "what we want to know if you saw them, or anyone, behaving out of the way at the wedding."

Ananya shakes her head. "No, I don't think so, *papa* and Shiva-*bhaiya* were talking about the business equity meeting the whole day, and then, Shiva-*bhaiya* had to ask her. Probably because it was only a fortnight away from my wedding, but I was a bit harsh on Shiva-*bhaiya*, even though I regretted it a lot," Ananya ended, "I always saw and thought of him as a family."

"Anything that happened out of the ordinary?" Inspector Ramanujan insists, "Mr Apte was attacked on the day of your engagement party, Mrs Rathi."

Ananya's face hardens, before crumpling up again, "I remember that a few days before the engagement party, I had called Shiva-*bhaiya* slow, because he was so preoccupied with things, even when he was in the house. other than that, only my dad and my uncle were busy, occupied with all the information about the Mehra equity deal." She stops, pausing for a breath, "I am sorry, but I do not remember anyone who could have been suspicious."

"He also came to the terrace," Ananya says, absent-mindedly, "Shiva-*bhaiya* never comes to the terrace. He prefers to either call me, to come down to the living room, or, he chooses to eat in the car instead."

"Was he afraid of heights?" the Inspector leans forward, "was Mr Apte afraid of heights?"

"Not really," Ananya says, "but I think he had seen something dangerous, some time ago. If I tried to ask him about it, he would just shake his head and go away. But it had been a few years since he has stepped foot onto the terrace."

Deputy Inspector Alam says nothing. Ananya continues, "I heard that he was either attacked on the terrace, or that he was dragged there?"

"Well, Mrs Rathi," Deputy Inspector Alam's next words are directed at Ananya Rathi, "we cannot say anything about it at the moment."

"Then why are you questioning me?" Ananya asks, "no one saw him go to the terrace on that day. None of us did."

"Even by those estimates," Deputy Inspector Alam's voice is soft, "that means you were the last person to see him alive, Mrs Ananya Rathi."

Ananya gapes.

"Did we not say that someone had him murdered?" she says, leaning away from the table, "I had never once thought of harming Shiva-*bhaiya*. A man died, and now you are trying to put the blame on me?"

"You misunderstand, Mrs Rathi," Deputy Inspector Alam says, but Ananya stands up, fuming.

"Thank you very much," she says stiffly, before walking out of the room.

⋈◈⋉

"So, what did you think?" Inspector Ramanujan asks, propping his feet onto the table, "is she innocent in these matters?"

"Not really, sir," Deputy Inspector Alam replies, "although I doubt how much she knows by herself, her husband *definitely* knows a lot more than he wants to let on."

"You sure?"

"He was the one to suggest the long drive," Deputy Inspector Alam says, "even Dushyant Chauhan admitted it. It was proposed to by Sooraj Rathi himself. Therefore, one needs to wonder, *did he know that something might happen?* Ananya has a history of being overtly sensitive to things, prone to bouts of hysteria. I wonder if he simply wanted to get both himself and Ananya out of the house, because he knew something might happen that day itself, when they were away from the house."

Inspector Ramanujan's eyes light up, "I *knew it*. I knew there was something that Sooraj Rathi was hiding. But what could it have been?"

"He's more involved than he is letting on, sir," Deputy Inspector Alam says, picking up a paperweight in his hands, "I wonder how he got married to Ananya Chauhan, of all people."

"Idle gossip again, Alam?" Ramanujan smiles, "go on, spit it out, whatever you are thinking."

"If Ananya's parents were looking for a husband for her, would it not make sense for them to get someone who moves in the same social circles as them?" Deputy Inspector Alam

86

asks, thoughtful, "Sooraj Rathi is rich, yes, but he has none of the pedigree that these families normally look for. He has no family to speak of, and the only address that we have of him belongs to his home here in Delhi, and his ancestral home in Hisar, Haryana."

Inspector Ramanujan turns to Deputy Inspector Alam, sharp, "Sooraj Rathi lived in Hisar?"

"The records say as much, sir," Deputy Inspector Alam waves a manila folder, "Born in Hisar, moved to Delhi at the age of six. He's been in and out of state-funded orphanages since then, until he struck it big as a business graduate, opening a small consulting firm, rapidly expanding it, fast enough to catch the eyes of even the most prestigious families in town."

"Families such as the Chauhan family," Inspector Ramanujan stands up, "one wonders how much of it is fiction, and how much of it is truth."

"A lot of it is fiction, sir," Deputy Inspector Alam says, "families such as the Chauhans and the Mehras, they marry their children both on accounts of the money of the other party, as well as the family—I mean, the pedigree of the bride or the groom. If anything, the family name nad prestige matters more to them than money, although a lot of it certainly would not be a problem."

"Which makes one wonder, how much of Sooraj Rathi do we know? He has no family to speak of, and yet he has moved into the Chauhan family mansion? No pedigree to speak of, no foreign university education, yet, he managed to become the son-in-law of Lata Diamonds."

"Suspicious, Alam, very suspicious." Inspector Ramanujan says, absent-minded, "everything is becoming more and more complicated by the hour."

"I wonder how much of it leads us to Hisar." Deputy Inspector Alam says, "both the Chauhan family, and the Mehra family are from Hisar, Haryana, and now, even Sooraj Rathi. No matter how you try to look at it, sir, I think the answer to all of this lies in Hisar."

Chapter 8

A CONFESSION

"Maybe if we bend the knees, and put the body in a foetal position?"

– A Death in the Gunj (2016)

"All rise."

Aditya Mehra would have never thought that he would be standing here, in a court, being accused of murder, conspiracy to commit murder, and, of course, drugs.

How did they manage to get that much information on me? he wonders, being pushed forward by the police officer, until his toes hit the wooden slats of the dock. *Ah, yes. Now I get questioned.*

He was someone who kept a lot of secrets, Aditya knew. Which is why he would wisely keep his mouth shut when questioned further. *there was no need to get on their wrong side. After all, Shiva Apte ended up being murdered.*

Of course, he was afraid. This would have happened eventually, but it still unsettled him; Aditya Mehra had never thought that he would have to be the one to pay someone for the murder of Shiva Apte. Twenty-five lakhs for the murder of Shiva Apte. Even *he* thought it was too low.

"Mr Mehra," The prosecution's lawyer, Mr Deshpande, stands up to face him, "would you care to explain the twenty-five lakhs that was wired from the offshore account in your name, to your cousin's account?"

Aditya cringes a little. The account had been a mistake. He was supposed to be putting away a little bit of his money every month in that account, but he had slipped, and for the past half a year, that account had been left to its own devices, in some offshore system. Not that he himself cared very much about the account, or about the money that his father had kept there. It was originally done to launder money under his name, and now Aditya himself used it to get money to murder Shiva Apte. He had met the man once, maybe twice. Liked him quite a lot, too. Aditya would be lying if he said that it had been easy for him to tell Vikram to murder Shiva Apte, but Apte had been interfering for a long time. Not to mention the growing unease between the Chauhans and the Mehras. The old man, Maan Singh, had become suspicious as of late. A disappointment, since Shiva had been really helpful in their little venture.

"The money in the offshore account can be accessed by members of my family. My father created the account in my name. I do not know about the day-to-day transactions made from that account." He says, aware of how stupid it sounds. The answer was well-rehearsed, but it all depended on the delivery of the lines. He had repeated them over and over in his mind, in the holding cell, even on the way to the court.

The prosecutor changes his way of questioning, "You were arrested with cocaine on you, three lakh rupees, in a nightclub. You sold cocaine to a plainclothes policeman, which would make bail highly improbable. You will go to prison for ten years either way, Mr Mehra. What is the point in denying the truth?"

He sighs. *They are getting on my nerves.* Going to prison was always a possibility for him. either for the embezzlement of money, or well, for conspiracy to commit murder. True, he had not expected it to be so soon, but Aditya Mehra was someone who was always prepared.

"The truth?" he doesn't know what the truth is, but he cenrtainky does not expect the truth to be here, in a courtroom of all places, "the truth is that I did not know what kind of money was in that account—"

"You knew, Mr Mehra!" Deshpande cuts him off, pointing an accusing finger towards him.

On the screen beside him, there is the text that Aditya had sent Vikram, the night that Shaiva Apte died. It had been sent from a prepaid phone, not even in his own name, but they had apparently found it.

I'm screwed.

"All rise."

Ananya surveyed the scene in front of her warily. In the dock, meant for the accused, stood Aditya Mehra, the boy she had known for years now, the youngest of the Mehra family. *Had she ever thought that this day would come? Being witness to a trial, involving the people that were the closest to her?* She knew Aditya Mehra, had known him since they were children. Although Lata Jewellers and Mehra Jewellers were both at odds with each other, Ananya and Aditya would spend time together at society events, parties where they were the youngest children around, with no one to supervise.

She shook her head. They were calling on him now. Ananya had never really been in a courtroom before, and indeed, never to witness a murder trial. *Conspiracy to commit murder. Ah well.* To her, all of them were the same. If Aditya Mehra had been the one to get her Shiva-*bhaiya* killed, Ananya was sure she would never forgive him.

They had pleaded not guilty in the hearing before this. Ananya was not present, but her father had been. Dushyant never really talked to her about these things, but ananya had begged him to tell her about the court proceedings, and so, he had invited himself to tea one afternoon, when Sooraj had been out of the house, and had told Ananya about the happenings of the court in the previous day.

Apparently, after they had pleaded not guilty, her father had momentarily stood up, before remembering is surroundings and coming back to his senses. He could not believe his ears anymore. Aditya Mehra had been accused and an inquiry had been held against him, for conspiring to murder Shiva Apte. The evidence pointed towards Aditya Mehra being the one behind all this, so why were they fighting it till the end? Did they really have no shame?

Ananya remembered everything that her father had told her, and then some more. The newspapers were filled with speculations about the person who had been behind this, the reasons why he did it, and some more. Aditya Mehra was being talked about, by every major newspaper in the city. And, although the share prices of Mehra Jewellers had fallen in the initial days following the breaking of this news, now everything seemed to be back on track, with their share prices *increasing,* instead of decreasing.

She could never really shake off the feeling that there was something that she was missing.

First, how did the Mehras know about the dates of the jewellery launch? They had their exhibition three days before the Chauhans, making fools out of the lot of them, even though the dates were kept secret until the announcement. But Mehra Jewellery knew when the announcement was going to take place, and released statements to the press mere hours before them; as a result, Lata Jewellery had taken a hit.

Ananya bites her bottom lip, frowning. *This was information known only to very few people in the company. I knew, simply because of my father. The company secrets being leaked to the competition should not be a cause of worry, however. Trade secrets are leaked all the time. Not every employee can be loyal until death.*

Except, of course, Shiva bhaiya. He was loyal, even in his death.

"I wonder how they came to know about the dates of the announcement of the jewellery exhibition." She wonders out loud, tapping her nails on the leather of her handbag. *And she wanted to know the answers. How did the competition get a hold of something that was to be confined within their own family?*

"Mr Mehra," The prosecution's lawyer, Mr Deshpande, stands up to face Aditya, "would you care to explain the twenty-five lakhs that was wired from the offshore account in your name, to your cousin's account?"

Ananya thinks that Aditya shrinks a little bit, before recomposing himself, "the money in the offshore account can be accessed by members of my family. My father created the account in my name. I do not know about the day-to-day transactions made from that account."

"The account had not been touched in the past six months, Mr Mehra," the lawyer turns on him, "the only time there had been any withdrawal made on that account in recent months, was when twenty-five lakhs were deposited into the account of Vikram Motwane, *your* cousin."

"Again, anyone in my family could have made that withdrawal," Aditya says, rubbing his hands over his face, "I am not the only one with any sort of access to that account."

"So, you mean to tell me that an account in *your name* is being run by other people?" Ananya should have known about Deshpande. He was a hawk. Somehow, the feeling of happiness, at seeing the person who had her Shiva-*bhaiya* killed, was diminished by her thoughts about the exhibition. She had texted her cousin, Ashish about it, but he had avoided her question, saying that he knew nothing of the exhibition, and even less about the plans of their own family.

This was going to be a problem.

"As I have said before," Aditya sounds frustrated, and Ananya remembers the many times that they had spent simply talking, in society events that made little sense to her anymore, "I do not maintain the account. Whatever happened, was not to my knowledge."

"You were arrested with cocaine on you, three lakh rupees, in a nightclub," Deshpande changes his way of examination, "you sold cocaine to a plainclothes policeman, which would make bail highly improbable. You will go to prison for ten years either way, Mr Mehra. What is the point in denying the truth?"

"The truth?" Aditya sounds frustrated, at the judicial system, at his own situation, "the truth is that I did not know what kind of money was in that account—"

"You knew, Mr Mehra!" Deshpande turns on him, and for a split second, Ananya can see a glimpse of something in Aditya's eyes, a mix of fear and terror and everything, "Your own text records are proof. You told Vikram Motwane, on the day of the attack made against Shiva Apte, if *the job* had been completed." He picks up a remote, and with a single click, a chat is projected onto a white screen, one that Ananya had not noticed before. *Really? How did I miss that?* On the screen was a single chat conversation,from Aditya to his cousin. Deshpande takes a look at Aditya, who has a stricken look on his face, "there you have it, Mr Mehra. Your evidence. You sent this text to Mr Motwane because you were inquiring about the job, were you not? The murder of Shiva Apte was the job that you wanted to know about. Whether or not it was handled well."

"Objection my lord," the lawyer for the defence stands up, bristling, "the prosecution cannot make assumptions."

"Sustained," the judge bangs his gavel lightly, "Mr Deshpande, you cannot be serious with this. Accusing the defendant is the police's job, not yours. Convict him through proper means, will you?"

"Fine, your honour," Deshpande takes a moment to gather himself, but does not look mollified at all, "Mr Mehra, are you close with your cousin?"

"He is my cousin," Aditya replies, "it is unbecoming if I do not maintain a good relationship with the members of my extended family."

"The Mehra jewellery business is family-owned, is it not?"

"Yes."

"However, Mr Mehra, your cousin took no part in the company's day-to-day workings. Would there be any need for you to maintain a good relationship with a distant cousin, simply because of family ties?"

"Objection, my lord, leading questions." The defence lawyer stands up again.

"Denied," the judge says, "objective questions are not leading questions."

"You win some, you lose some, counsel," Deshpande says, quietly, and even though the defence bristles, there is nothing they can do about it. Aditya Mehra would have to keep his mouth shut, now.

"I maintain good relationships with the members of my extended family simply because they are family, Mr Deshpande," Aditya leans forward, the smile on full display. *There it was. That smile meant that he was in control. No matter what happened now, it would be by his rules, and no one else's,* "I am sorry, if you do not recognise the difference between business relationship and simply being a good person."

Ananya wanted to laugh out loud, in the middle of the courtroom. *Being a good person? The man who had someone else killed, just for money?*

Deshpande bristles at the jab, but continues, "so, you admit that you were close to people of your family, despite there not being any sort of business relations?"

"I said I was cordial, sir. I never said the word 'close'." Aditya says, face morphing into something hard and brittle.

"The cocaine that you sold, Mr Mehra," Deshpande leans in, "is in the hands of the Narcotics Bureau. They will place you in jail, be sure of it. and you would still be so stubborn about admitting your own guilt in the murder of Mr Shiva Apte?"

"Objection my lord," the defence lawyer ises again, "the two trials are separate and cannot be used to influence my client."

"Sustained," the judge says, now irritable, "Mr Deshpande, I didn't know you were a new law graduate."

"That will be all, my lord," Mr Deshpande says, stepping away from the dock, "no more questions for Mr Mehra."

Chapter 9

BACK AGAIN

"History, Stephen said, is a nightmare from which I am trying to awaken."

– James Joyce

Dushyant was back here again. This time, voluntarily, or perhps involuntarily, but without any choice of his own in the matter, as usual. Inspector Ramanujan had asked him to come down to the station, again, for another round of interrogations, and he had complied. Not that he had much to do, either way. With the mess concerning the exhibition and the share market, he was already in hot water when it concerned anything to do with the company, and by extension, this investigation. His father had not been happy with the way that the Mehras had disrupted their plans for the jewellery exhibition, the new collection having to be delayed for another month, for fear of the public and the media taking their designs as nothing but a cheap copy of the designs that the Mehras had created. Dushyant had seen the pictures of the Mehra exhibition, and had indeed been taken aback at the similarity between their own designs and the designs made by the Mehras.

Which worried him further. When his father had been berating Angad, responsible for the engineering and design aspect of their production process, Dushyant had been outside the room, just listening in on the conversation. He could not shake off the sensation that there was something that he had been missing, something important, but even as his wife Damini threw him a contemptuous glance before sweeping in into his father's room with a tray of tea—he knew there was something that they had all been withholding from him.

When Dushyant had been a boy, or even when Dushyant had been a young man, most of his life had been spent away from his family. When he had been a boy of six, his health had failed, and as a result, his father sent him away frm their ancestrla home in Hisar, Haryana, to Delhi, at their cousin's place, where Dushyant remained for quite some years, being more accustomed to the house in Delhi than the house back in Hisar. The Delhi house was small, cramped, with too little space for too many people—his aunt and uncle, his cousins, the servants—even though the house had been bigger than normal for Delhi standards, Dushyant remembers it as small, as confined spaces occupied with laughter, always, incessant. Or maybe his cousins never did like the concept of being far apart from each other, when they were family. But in Hisar, in the old ancestral house of the Chauhan family that had been their home for generations, Dushyant had been left alone mostly, perhaps because of his frail health, or when he grew older, as someone who had been brought up outside the confines of the family, thus becoming someone foreign. He could feel it every time he entered a room, and they would fall silent, at the calculated distance the servants maintained, that June when he had returned to his father's home, eighteen years old. By then, the Chauhans were already moving to Delhi permanently, and the estate that they had bought a few years prior, one that Dushyant had never really seen, despite living for twelve years in the city itself. His aunt and uncle had moved away by then, to England, and if they had not moved, Dushyant would have remained at their house for a little while longer. The south Delhi bungalow that he had once thought of as cramped and uncomfortable had become a welcome refuge by the time that he had walked back into his father's home in Hisar, Haryana.

And now, he was here. In this police station, waiting for the two policemen to come and interrogate him for the third time. Dushyant felt exhausted. He had already been interrogated once in the morning, by Anshul, of all people.

He knew his status in his family's dynamic, even if he never liked to acknowledge it. *After all, who would like to stare their own misfortune in the face?* His father refused to talk to him on occasion. His mother, the only person who made him feel as though he was a part of her family, was dead and gone, long before any of this mess with Shiva.

And his wife and daughter? Ananya was married to a good man. Or at least, as good as a man that Dushyant had known him to be. Sooraj had been respectful, and courteous. He was a good man, as much as Dushyant could see. Ananya was also happy. Damini, on the other hand, had always chafed in the role of his wife, subserviency not in her innate nature. When his sister-in-law had been alive, she had struggled for years, although Dushyant had never been aware of this. He had been a failure of a man. Both as a father, and as a husband. Even as a son.

"Mr Chauhan," the unsmiling face of a young constable enters the room, "I'm sorry, but both Inspector Ramanujan and Deputy Inspector Alam are not here. You are free to leave, although you may be summoned again, soon."

"They are not here?" Dushyant's confusion may have surprised the young constable too, "but I was given a summons for this afternoon."

"Yes, you were," the constable says, "but both the Inspectors were called away on an emergency."

"Emergency?"

"I don't know all the details," the constable says, mulling it over, "but something to do with Hisar."

"Our ancestral home?" Dushyant mutters, low enough that the constable does not hear him. *What were they doing in Hisar. More importantly, what were they going to find in Hisar?*

Hisar was their ancestral home, a place which he had left, back when he had been a boy of six. Maan Singh had not been too keen on the idea, but Dushyant's mother had convinced him, saying that it would be good for his health to go to a big city like Delhi, where they had hospitals, large enough for Dushyant to be taken care of well. *He would be better off there,* his mother had told his father, *there are so many big hospitals in Delhi, Dushyant would be well taken care of, with my sister and her husband. They love him a lot.*

There are hospitals in Hisar too, his father had replied, and it would have ended there, had it not been for his mother, again.

Send him to Delhi, Anshul's father, she had said, almost pleading. It was a look that she wore often, especially when trying to talk to his father about him. the use of his eldest brother's name was also something his mother did, to make the anger a little less. It seemed that Maan Singh Chauhan despised his youngest son with every passing day, and all his affection went towards his oldest.

Fine, his father had said, waving a hand. *Let the brat go to Delhi.*

His father had relented that day, but Dushyant still remembered the fond smile on her face when he had been packing his bags, eager to go out and see the world. Hisar was a village back then, and Dushyant was a big fish in a small pond. With all the precocious nature of a six-year-old, who knew nothing about the world, Dushyant wanted to move away from his stuffy old house, into a new place. His mother had looked at him then, with a curious sadness in her eyes, as though she was losing a child.

When his father hated him, Dushyant turned to his mother, and his mother took him in, her favourite child. Frail since a young age, Dushyant was sent off to Delhi to live with his aunt and uncle. There, he attended school, went to the university hospital for regular check-ups on his health. His mother never visited him.

"Please tell Inspector Ramanujan that I had been here," he says,

The family mansion was imposing, even at a distance. Dushyant had never really thought of it as intimidating before, but this morning, driving his car, he has an insane thought. *What if all this had been done by someone I know?*

Despite being the youngest of the Chauhan family, Dushyant was never really a part of the whole picture. *I assume that's part of the job, really, when you move away from your parents fo twelve years, there are bound to be some sort of distances between you and the rest of the family members, sometimes gulfs too big to bridge over.*

"Damini," he calls for his wife, as soon as he enters through the double doors, "Damini, a cup of tea, in my room."

It's still early evening, a time when his wife sits for hours with her books, and he knows she's going to be angry with him for disturbing her precious few moments of peace. *I will take those odds.*

Their room is empty, save for Damini's various books on physics on the floral bedspread. Dushyant sits on his chair, untying the oxford knot of his tie. Damini would be here soon, and he had some things that he needed to talk to her about. Damini was much more capable than him, she would be much more competent, in handling such matters. Dushyant felt as though he was underwater, with no source of light in the dark depths. *What happened in those years that I was away, and why does no one seem to care about it anymore? When I returned home after spending twelve years in Delhi, my father never talked to me about the things that transpired in my absence. And they never really went back to the Hisar house, instead relocating to Delhi to expand their diamond business, two years after I returned to Haryana.*

No, none of it made sense to him. Maybe it would make sense to his wife.

She walked into the room with perhaps a bit more urgency than usual, hir in a severe bun rather than a loose updo. Dushyant was reminded of the scales of justice in his university, in front of the school of Law. She looked like that.

Sometimes, when he's a bit less selfish, usually at nights, he wonders what would have happened if he had not married her, right out of university. Dushyant had effectively ruined Damini's life, simply by marrying her and yoking the burden of the family upon her still-slender shoulders. She had been a gold medallist in Physics, and far smarter than him.

"Anshul bhai seems worried," she says by way of an introduction, setting the cup on the table, "he kept trying to talk to me, even went to the kitchen on occasion. I do not know what he is thinking, but it cannot be something good."

"Anshul *bhai?*" Dushyant had never seen his brother enter the kitchen, not willingly. And to go to the kitchen to ask Damini—no, there must be something there, "do you think he is trying to keep tabs on you?"

"Most likely," Damini perches herself on the edge of the bed, "he is not a stupid man, you know. All this moving around, in the company car—talking to Inspector Ramanujan and the Deputy Inspector, you think no one notices all this?"

"I had a summons," Dushyant makes a weak protest, but she cuts him off.

"Then do not take the company car, and if you haveto go. You still get a handsome salaray from the company, use that money to get yourself a cab. You think they do not relay every bit of information to Anshul bhaiya and *baba?*"

"They do?" Dushyant is not a stupid man, he known that there has to be some sort of information relay involved, for his family to know everything about their own members. But to be spied upon by his brother, that was something that disturbed him. *Did Anshul bhai keep tabs on me from the beginning? Or was this a recent development?*

He takes a sip of the tea, dark and bitter, the way he likes it, "what did Anshul bhaiya want to know about?"

"The fact that you have been going to the police," Damini replies, a frown on her face, "I presume they already know about everything, and they just want to confirm it. going to the police station so many times, even if it is at a summons by the Inspector himself, is not a good look in the eyes of this family."

"What do you propose I do?" Dushyant asks, "I cannot refuse a summons, because they might show up with a warrant—who am I fooling, they *will* show up with a warrant. Inspector Ramanujan and the Deputy Inspector must be under pressure from the headquarters of police to close the case as quickly as possible."

"Let me think of something," Damini tells him, "Oh, Sooraj came by today too."

"Sooraj?" Dushyant's surprise at the sudden visit from his son-in-law makes Damini frown again, "without Ananya?"

"Yes, I thought it was strange too," she confesses, "he acted quite strangely. Even though *baba* himself asked him to stay for lunch, he made paper-thin excuses about being at the firm for the day, if he had to be at the firm so urgently, then why bother to come over to the house? It is not as though our house is walking distance from his firm. It would have been easier for him, in fact, to just go back to his house for lunch, instead of spending time with us."

"He may have just wanted to be here, you know," he defends weakly, even though the suspicion has already crept into his mind. *What was Sooraj doing? Did Ananya know about this?*

"I asked Ananya," Damini says, "she did not have any idea about Sooraj's coming to the house. It seems as though he is hiding something."

"Hiding something?" now it is Dushyant's turn to be incredulous, "come on, Damini, if that was indeed the case, then Ananya would have told us, would she not?"

"I am wondering if Ananya knows herself."

Chapter 10

HISAR

"It is better to be hated for what you are than to be loved for what you are not."

– Andre Gide, Autumn Leaves

Hisar was warm this time of the year. Deputy Inspector Alam scrambles down from the police jeep, that had now screeched to a halt in from of the old Chauhan mansion. Formerly great, it was now a dilapidated affair, and he swayed back on forth on his boots, unconsciously, to make sure his hunting boots fit better.

"Seems like no one lives here anymore," Inspector Ramanujan says, "why are you moving back and forth like that?"

"There could be snakes," Deputy Inspector Alam says, "we probably should not be going in there so recklessly."

"Recklessly? Alam, both of us have hunting boots on, there is backup if we request it, you think this is reckless?" his superior sighs, "we must do something about that general fear of snakes of yours. What would your wife say?"

"Fortunately, I am not yet married, sir."

"Fortunately?" Inspector Ramanujan raises an eyebrow, "do you mean to say that you are one of those people who think of marriage as a trap?"

"My wife would be displeased with me if she had to get rid of every snake that we encounter, by herself." Deputy Inspector Alam says, voice dry.

Inspector Ramanujan laughs, and so do the two officers that accompanied them, and Alam rubs the back of his neck, suddenly bashful.

"Have there been any tenants in this house?" Inspector Ramanujan asks the two officers, "the records do not show anything, but there could be squatters in the area."

"Sir, we do not know about squatters," the heavily-accented constable replies, hitting the floor with his stick rhythmically, "but we cannot rule out the possibility of it, at least not now. The Chauhan family was not large, but they were very influential. Them moving away to Delhi did have a lot of effect on the local economy as well, and not a positive one."

"Did the Mehras live nearby?" Deputy Inspector Alam asks, "both of the families were from Hisar, so it makes some sense that they would be nearby, given the area of the village."

The other constable, a considerably older man, with a drooping moustache, responds, "well, the Mehras lived about three miles away from here, and they were not a small family. There were Mehras everywhere in Hisar. Still are, if you look hard enough."

"What do you mean?" Deputy Inspector Alam turns around, "what do you mean 'if you look hard enough'?"

"Who are you looking for?"

The sound comes from a corner, and the four of them turn at once, senses on high alert. It is a five-year old boy, with big eyes and dirty hair, evidently living in the house. *Well, so much for no inhabitants.* "Are you here to turn us out?"

"Boy," Inspector Ramanujan says softly, "where are your parents?"

"They're inside," the boy replies, "but my name isn't *boy*. It's Ram."

"Well, Ram," the younger constable replies, take us to your parents."

The boy gives a furtive look around the corner, and turns to the four of them, confusion writ large on his face, "they are not here."

"You just said that they were here."

"But they aren't." He insists, "I cannot see them."

"Tell your parents that we were here to talk about the Chauhans," Deputy Inspector Alam says, "you can shout it too, if you want. No one is going to tell you anything."

"Shout it?" the boy's eyes go wide, "*ma*! The policemen told me they are here for the Chauhan thing!"

Inspector Ramanujan looks at Deputy Inspector Alam, eyebrows furrowed. "And if they are criminals on run from the law?"

"Criminals on run from the law do not tend to keep a five-year old in their midst, sir," Deputy Inspector Alam says, "besides, his eyes are focused. Wide, but focused. He is not on drugs, neither is he worried about anything."

Inspector Ramanujan says nothing, as two people cautiously make their way down a flight of stairs, a man and a woman, both of them looking extremely nervous. The woman looked as though she would vomit at any moment.

The old house must have peeling lead paint. The looks of lead poisoning had already settled into her skin.

"Come into the courtyard, sir," the man says, "we are— illegal settlers here, as you can see."

"Illegal immigrants?"

"No, no," the look on the woman's face is wild, distressed, "there are not many places to go, for people like us."

"What do you mean?"

The two of them look at each other, and then at the four policemen. Inspector Ramanujan muses something, and says, "the two of you, wait outside. We will finish shortly."

"Yes sir." And when the constables are gone, the woman holds her presumed husband's hand, "we are not from the same caste, you see, and if anyone knows—"

"How long have you been living here?" Inspector Ramanujan asks, "was your son born here?"

"A year," the man says, "we were tired of being on the run, and there was this house—"

"There was no one apart from you when you moved in?" Deputy Inspector Alam asks now, "this whole house was empty?"

"Yes, sir." The man takes a look at his wife, "please, sir, we cannot go to the hospital. My wife is very sick. let us go to another city, sir."

Inspector Ramanujan rises to his feet, "you have to come with us to Delhi. This house is currently the focus of a murder investigation and trial."

☙◈❧

Ananya was sitting alone in her home's drawing-room, drinking a cup of tea. The tea itself was expensive, the sweet aroma of it almost overpowering in the otherwise empty drawing-room. Sooraj, her husband, did not like scents, especially overpowering ones. While at her home, the evening *aarti* was a sort of comforting regular occurrence, her big house, lifeless and empty in the evenings, made her feel oddly out of place. Ananya had never really liked the smell of incense either, but her mother walking into her room for the *aarti* was something that was part of her regular routine. And now, it was all disrupted.

Sooraj had gone to their house, Ananya's family home, without telling her. Ananya wasn't the sort of person who demanded to know everything from her husband; although she knew some people who were, especially in her own circles, Ananya always liked to have trust in the person who understood her the most. Even beyond her parents, Sooraj was the one who knew about her anxiety disorder, and the panic episodes, that she often kept hidden from her parents.

Her cousin had texted her in the afternoon, about her husband coming to the house. Ashish often joked around a lot, but on this occasion, he seemed tensed, almost wary of her husband. Ananya was not exactly sure what made him think this, but she had called her mother, just in case. Her mother had said nothing about Sooraj visiting, and neither had her father. Ashish's words still bothered her, however, the tone with which he had written, *did you know, that Sooraj is in our house right now?*

Sent around lunchtime. The Chauhan family mansion was further away from Sooraj's office than his own home, and he still made the trip to the house. If he had wanted to go visit her parents, shouldn't he have asked her to accompany him? Ananya did not like this. The suspicion, the subterfuge—all of it made no sense to her, not in this matter, not anymore. She would talk to her husband directly.

Her phone vibrates. Another text alert from her cousin. Ananya sighs, before unlocking her phone screen, but before she can read the text, her phone starts ringing. A call from Ashish.

"What?" she asks, a bit irritated, "I was just going to read the message, why did you have to call?"

"Are you aware of everything that your husband does?" her cousin asks, sharply, "Why is our grandfather asking me if I know anything about Sooraj?"

"Grandfather?" Ananya cannot keep the shock from her voice as she repeats Ashish's words, "why would *Dadaji* ask about Sooraj?"

"He thinks someone in the house asked Sooraj to visit unannounced," Ashish says, and Ananya has to strain her ears to hear him over the noise of cars. *Is he calling me from outside the house? He should be back home by now, it is late in the evening.* "Did you do it?"

"Do what?" Ananya asks, too focused on the background noises to listen properly to Ashish's words, "what do you mean?"

"Your fiancé—husband, now—visited the house and was asking questions." Ashish sounds both bitter as well as furtive, and in all her years of knowing her cousin, he had never sounded like this. She shook her head, because Ashish was speaking again, "Ananya, I just found out something about Sooraj, and well, he had a motive."

"Motive? You are beginning to talk like one of those policemen, Ashish," Ananya says, angry, somehow. *How dare he imply that my husband had some sort of motive? In what?* "What motive? For what? Sooraj married me because he loves me, and that is all there is to it. nothing more, nothing less."

"This is about the marriage, Ananya," Ashish sounds more urgent now, "You met him at the club, right? And a friend introduced the two of you?"

"Yes, but how does that help here?" Ananya bristles, "yes, I met him at the club, and a friend introduced the two of us. He did fall in love with *me,* and not the friend."

"Which club did you meet him at?"

"*Divine,*" Ananya blurts out, the memories of that night when she had met Sooraj blurry, "but I do not see how that is important now—"

She stops. Because, Ananya remembers the friend that had introduced the two of them.

"Vikram Motwane, right?" Ashish says, "one of my friends is a regular at *Divine.* She remembers the night you met Sooraj, mostly because she ended up in the hospital afterwards."

"Hospital?"

"Drugs. Cocaine, to be specific," Ashish replies, the sound of the cars increasing, "she bought from Aditya Mehra that night, and ended up in the hospital. Almost died. She remembers what happened until he bought the drugs from Aditya, after which, her memory is gone. Wiped out."

"And what does she remember, this friend of yours?" Ananya asks, "if he remembers anything at all?"

"Aditya asked Vikram Motwane to introduce you to Sooraj." Ashish says, his voice far too calm for Ananya's mind, which was in shambles, "Vikram introduced the two of you, mostly because he knew you, and because Sooraj paid him to do it."

"Sooraj?" Ananya stands up in shock, "what the hell are you talking about?"

"If I didn't have proof, I would not be telling you this, Ananya, I am not stupid." Ashish says, "I'm sending you something right now. It's a video, that my friend took that night in the club. She's already drunk at this point, so the video is a bit shaky, but it is there. She was taking a video of the bartender, and ended up including the three of them, Vikram, Aditya, and Sooraj in the frame."

"Fine," Ananya replies, "still doesn't prove anything about this 'motive' that you keep speaking of. He could have seen me from afar, and decided that he liked me, in which case, your ideas and conclusions are bullshit."

Ashish sighs, "Ananya, if he really wanted to meet you because he liked you, would he have paid Vikram Motwane of all people to introduce you two?"

Ananya bites her fingernails, "I want to talk to this friend of yours. Who is she?"

"Rafiya—are you sure you want to meet her?" *Of all the things my brother could get emotional about, it's this girl.* Ananya sighs.

"Ashish, I am not your parents, neither am I her parents," she says, placating, "I'll keep your secret. You took her to the hospital that night, right? You didn't come back home on the night I met Sooraj. I wanted to talk to you about him, but you did not return until the next morning."

Ashish is silent, which can only mean one thing—she's correct. "I'll call her in the morning, Ashish," she says, softly, "I actually liked the two of you together."

"Don't be too hard on her, Ananya," her brother sounds remorseful over the phone line, "I'm the reason why she was there in that club that night. It was a—well, since I've told you so much, I can tell you this now, it was a suicide attempt."

"A suicide attempt?"

"She thought she was pregnant, Ananya, and I refused to believe anything. Of course, at the hospital she found out it was nothing, but even then, she wanted to commit suicide, because of me."

"Understood," Ananya says, "what do you think this means? If Sooraj paid Vikram Motwane to introduce the two of us, and potentially to marry me, what does that mean?"

"It means that he wanted to enter our house—ah!" Ashish yells over the phone, and there is a sickening crunch, before the line goes dead.

Chapter 11

ASHISH CHAUHAN

"All happy families are alike; each unhappy family is
unhappy in its own way."

– Leo Tolstoy, Anna Karenina

"Next witness for the Prosecution, Ashish Chauhan."

Ashish doesn't say anything, being led up to the steps.
Ananya watches her brother, wary. He looks tired. Ashish
always looks tired now, a far cry from the carefree boy that
she had grown up around. *Shova-bhaiya passing must have
meant a lot to him, too.*

"Mr Chauhan," Prosecutor Deshpande says, "what do
you remember about the events leading to Mr Shiva Apte's
death?"

"It was the day of Ananya's engagement party," Ashish
replies, "I don't think I remember much from the day itself,
but Sooraj had taken Ananya out for a drive, when the
incident happened. They were about an hour—two hours?
Away from the house, when her Dushyant *chacha* called her,
and told her to return. She had no idea."

"Sooraj Rathi took her for a drive?"

"Yeah, he said that Ananya was feeling stifled with the
wedding preparations, so he took her out. Dushyant *chacha*

protested, but he relented after a little while. He really can't say no to Ananya."

"What else do you remember from that day, Mr Chauhan?"

"Nothing—nothing much, really," Ashish stutters, "there was a lot of commotion that day."

"Very well, Mr Chauhan," Prosecutor Deshpande replies, stepping away, "you will be called again, to take the stand."

ෲ◈ౡ

"Ashish? Ashish, can you hear me? Shit!" Ananya swears, frantically dialling the police, "hello? Yes, I think my brother was in an accident? His phone number is—please, you need to find him quickly—"

The house is silent now. Ananya has called her parents, all of whom have told her that it would be the best, for her to stay where she was, for now. *There's a resemblance to this. To how Shiva bhaiya was murdered. Even then, I had to go to the hospital late at night.*

Her phone rings. Ananya pounces on the device, swiping to accept the call with trembling fingers. *Just hope it is not the worst. Hope for the best, prepare for the worst.*

"Ananya," her father calls her, "Ashish is not hurt as much as we had thought, but it is not going to be easy, either. The incoming vehicle would have hit his car on the side, but he swerved at the right time, and they hit his car in the front instead. Fortunately, the airbags activated and he was rescued soon."

Ananya had not realised that she was crying. "Did they see who was driving the car? The one that ran into his car?

116

Was there a CCTV camera anywhere nearby? Is there a way to find out how he was hit?"

"Calm down," her father laughs, tired, "they're looking for more information right now, but all we know is that he was hit while driving through a very dark road. They're looking into it right now."

"So, there's nothing we can find about the person who tried to kill him?"

"The car was rented, and this is all we could find," Dushyant says, "your uncle is beyond himself right now. You should come to the house tomorrow, if you can."

"Shouldn't you tell her once?" Ananya regrets saying anything, the moment the words come out of her mouth, "sorry, shouldn't have said anything."

"No, no," her father sighs, "we should tell her. But the moment she steps into the hospital, your grandfather is going to throw a fit, as will your uncles. They already were angry with Ashish, imagine if she comes to visit him."

"Don't worry about it, *Papa*," ananya replies, "I'll talk to her tomorrow about it, and she might have already heard all about it from the newspapers."

"Hmm, let's see how this works out." Her father sighs, "putting so much pressure on the poor boy. God knows what would have happened tonight."

Her father pauses for a second, and then says again, "Wait, is Sooraj at home?"

"Sooraj?" ananya pauses. *Do I tell my father everything Ashish told me today? But what if all he said was a mistake? We can't trust Rafiya. And he could be mistaken about Sooraj,* "yeah, he's back. He's in the shower, now."

"Bring him around too, yeah?" her father says, "oh wait, the doctor is coming out. Ashish is out of danger."

"Really?" Ananya squeals, "he's, okay?"

"He will be okay, just needs to be put on observation for a bit." Her father reassures her, "don't worry about things here anymore, your mother and I are here. We'll take care of it. Sooraj must be tired now."

The phone disconnects, and Ananya sits in the dark for a while. *Why was Sooraj not here?* He had texted her three hours ago, something about being stuck at work, but he always called her, if he was going to be late. Why had he not called her?

The bell rings, and she jumps. *Sooraj. Of course, it was Sooraj, her husband. Who else would it be? Everything Ashish had told her was an exaggeration. He never thought of her that way. He never had a motive. He loved her. He loved her, and he never paid anyone to—*

"Ananya?"

Ananya stares at her husband. Sooraj had always been attractive, with the high cheekbones and strong brows, but in the flickering light of her drawing room, he looks odd. As though he had been approaching her for something, and had been thwarted, almost.

"Yes? Sorry, my mind was on something else." She mutters, "work was bad today, I presume?"

"Yeah," he yawns, stretching, "had to work overtime tonight, and have to go in early tomorrow, too. I wish I could take a day off, honestly."

"I wish you could, too," Ananya says, adding softly, "we haven't been anywhere since the wedding. Haven't even gone on a honeymoon, you know."

"Sorry," he smiles, "but we were told about that. Don't go out of the city. Inspector's orders."

Ananya smiles. *He was funny.* "Should I get you dinner?"

"Dinner?" he thinks about it for a moment, "no, I am not really hungry, darling. I'll just take a shower and go to bed. Have you eaten?"

"Me? Yes," she lies, "I've eaten dinner."

"Then go to sleep quickly," he kisses her forehead, handing her his waistcoat, "i'll be a few minutes."

Ananya smiles, running her hands over the fabric of the waistcoat. She liked the fabric, a nice blue pinstripe that Sooraj had made, just because she liked the blue pinstripe material. *He isn't like that. Ashish had been overreacting.*

"Ananya?"

"Hm?" she looks up, confused, "did you say something?"

"I said, do you need to tell me something?" Sooraj looks at her, tilting his head, "you seem awfully lost in thought there."

"Me? Oh, no, nothing of the sort." Ananya laughs, pushing him lightly, "go wash up, I'll be there soon."

When he leaves, she runs her hands over the fabric once, twice, thrice. That tear on the corner, marked black with soot. *Why would Sooraj's pristine coat be stained with soot?* A slight burnt smell from the piece of clothing, acrid. *Smoke? Burnt flesh?*

Most of all, that stain on the right pocket of his waistcoat, that's something Ananya knew.

Blood.

Chapter 12

AN ACCIDENT

"There is a luxury in self-reproach. When we blame ourselves, we feel that no one else has a right to blame us. It is the confession, not the priest, that gives us absolution."

– Oscar Wilde, The Picture of Dorian Gray

Inspector Ramanujan was at his wit's end. They had been working on this case for about three weeks now, closing in the fourth, and yet, there was nothing concrete that he could find out about the assault and murder, and who was behind it all, playing them on strings, like puppets, eager to do their bidding. If looked at from an objective viewpoint, most of the evidence, almost all of it, if he was being correct, pointed towards Aditya Mehra being the person to do so.

And yet—

He cannot shake off the feeling that they were missing something. *What was it?*

Now, standing in the dimly-lit interrogation room of the Hisar police station, he can understand better. It was not Aditya Mehra; in fact, it was not the Mehras at all. they had been moving in circles, trying to pin this on either the Mehra family or the Chauhan family; whichever fit better.

"Sir," Deputy Inspector Alam holds up a file, "the statements."

"Oh, right, the statements." Inspector Ramanujan takes the file from him, "did we get the signatures of the family that was living there'

"Yes, sir," Deputy Inspector Alam flips open the file, pointing to two signatures, scrawled in black ink, "they readily complied once we said that they would me moved to Delhi once they gave their statements. From what I can gather, they were living here in fear."

"That much is evident, Alam," Inspector Ramanujan leafs through the pages, "you have taken the statements of the rest of the villagers here?"

"Most of them were pretty unwilling to talk, given the police badge, but of the few who did, there are some bits of information that I found particularly interesting." Deputy Inspector Alam draws up a chair, sitting, "both the Mehras and the chauhans were once on very good terms."

"That doesn't make a lot of sense, given their very eminent animosity," Inspector Ramanujan muses, twirling a stray paperweight in his hands, "but I have heard worse turns in relationships between families."

Deputy Inspector Alam turns another page, flicking to a sentence at the very bottom, "Here, sir. I think this explains it better."

"What do you mean?" Inspector Ramanujan, slightly irritated now, looks at the sentence pointed out, "this does not signify anything."

"It does if you think of the timeline, sir."

"The timeline—ah." The inspector looks at his junior, setting down the paperweight, "well, doesn't this bring the investigation to another direction."

—Ashish was, thankfully, out of danger. Ananya had stayed beside his bed for three days before he had opened his eyes; her whole family had been overjoyed, but for some reason, the ecsasty never really reached her. There was a reason for it, of course, but she was not willing to put a name to it, not yet, at least. She had talked to her brother's girlfriend too, who was inconsolable, but the presence of her grandfather ensured that Rafiya would not be able to take a step inside the hospital premises, as long as Maan Singh Chauhan was present.

She had the video on her brother's laptop, instead of her own, too paranoid to even think about downloading the video sent to her on her personal phone. *Sooraj was right, when he married me. I am too paranoid for my own good.*

Still, nothing really took away from the fact that what she had seen on her husband's shirt the night of her brother's accident, was blood. Blood soaking the fabric, almost as though from a fresh wound. He had not touched her since that incident, and a part of her wondered if it was to avoid being caught by her. Sooraj's work was not dangerous, nothing that would warrant a wound. A very deep one, if the winces that she had heard from Sooraj the following morning were anything to go by. For the sake of her own sanity, Ananya had pretended to ignore them. nothing came out of excessive worrying.

For now, there was the matter of the video. While the quality of it was bad, well enough for a handheld phone, but given the fact that the videographer was under the influence at the moment of recording, there was an understandable amount of shaking. However, she could make out the three people clearly: Vikram Motwane, Aditya Mehra, and of course, her husband, Sooraj Rathi. *Why did he not come up to me himself? What was going on in his mind? Why did he have to involve the Mehras and their cousin, of all people?*

The truth was that none of the evidence would be presentable in court. She could drag Sooraj down, and litigate him to an inch of his life, but Ananya knew that all her conclusions from the video were mere implications. She needed something more concrete, to be able to leave Sooraj, as well as this marriage, behind her. If her suspicions were true, and he was involved in Ashish's accident, she would not forgive him, nor would she forgive herself. But to do so, she needed more proof. She needed to be able to prove that he was linked to her brother's accident.

If she took the video to court as is, the first question they would ask would be, *are you sure he had ill intentions? Or was he just shy and wanted to ask a friend to introduce the two of you?*

But she had never really heard from Vikram Motwane since the night that he had introduced the two of them, and nor was he invited to the wedding. In fact, he was the one who had attached Shiva bhaiya. Ananya suddenly felt sick to her stomach. *Was Sooraj always like this?* She would never be able to trust another person again, for as long as she lived. *Most of all, I would no longer be able to trust another man.* Did he know this? When he was asking for her hand in marriage, did he always have a goal in mind?

She was back at the old mansion, where she had been born and raised and had known it all her life, but this time, it felt a little different. With Ashish's accident, it felt as though the entire Chauhan family had fallen into despair. She was not angry. Ashish was the only son of the house, the one expected to carry on the Chauhan name, into larger countries, bigger markets. Her father and uncles always had an eye towards the world, and Ashish, being the oldest son, was the person on whose shoulders the entire responsibility fell. In that respect, she was lucky indeed, to be able to spend most of her life without much in the way of worries, regarding the family business.

"What happened? Is Sooraj at the office?" her father opens the doors for her, "you were here only last week."

"Sooraj has already gone to the office." Ananya replies, short, "I needed to tell you something about the accident."

"The accident?" her father looks around the house, furtively, as though looking for people who might eavesdrop in on their conversation, "what do you know?"

"Who has the case?" Ananya asks, walking towards the staircase, "it is not murder, so I doubt Inspector Ramanujan would be involved."

"There is no official case yet. Of course, the traffic division is looking into the matter, but since there were no security cameras in that location, it would be a bit difficult to find out the person who crashed their car into Ashish," her father says, following her, "but why are you asking about this?"

"I think I have an idea," Ananya waves a hand dismissively, "but that does not matter, at least for now. How did they find out that the car that crashed into Ashish's was a rental car? There was only Ashish's SUV in the scene. How did we find out that the car was a rented one?"

The two of them make their way to Ananya's room, and Ananya flings the doors open, walking up to her old bed and putting her bag on the table next to it; her father closes the door behind him, "there was a numberplate on it. the number was a commercial one, and by the time that Ashish had been in surgery, they had tracked the number to a commercial car, registered at a car rental."

"So, the actual car is still out there somewhere?" Ananya inquires, "does the criminal still have it?"

"They found the car, abandoned, in a pound, the next day." her father shakes her head, "there is little possibility of finding out who the person was, the one who rented the car."

"They should have a receipt at the rental shop, if the person rented it under their name, but that possibility is ruled out, almost immediately." Ananya bites her nails, "no one would be so stupid as to rent a car under their own name, especially if they were going to crash it into someone else's car only hours later."

"The booking was make online," her father clarifies, "there are no traces."

Ananya turns to look at him, "of course there are. There have to be ways of figuring that out."

"I mean, there could be—why are you so obsessed with this?" her father asks, "you were never really involved, not like this. Why are you so interested in this case?"

"Never mind that," Ananya waves a hand, and to her surprise, her father backs down, leaning back against the wall, "did the police find anything in the car?"

"Blood, but they don't have another sample to check it against, so for now, it's just languishing in storage."

"They could trace the IP from which the rent transaction was made, and for the blood—" Ananya was biting her nails again, "—for the blood, I think I should talk to the police myself."

"Ananya," her father's tone is soft, soothing, the one that he used only when Ananya was close to a panic attack, "what do you know?"

She sighs, rubbing her face with the palm of her hands. *They are going to have their hearts broken.* Her parents loved her husband so much, Ananya remembers them being overjoyed to find out that she was dating Sooraj Rathi, and even more enthusiastically planning their wedding. "I was on the phone with Ashish."

"On the—"

"Just before the accident." She says, ignoring the stricken look on her father's face, "I heard the crash over the phone."

"You heard the call?" her father stands up, "why did you not tell us?"

"It would be easier to keep the truth from you, than to tell you the truth," Ananya says, "Ashish was convinced that someone else was behind the whole thing. The murder, the wedding, everything."

"Ashish was wrong!" her father almost shouts, "the person who hired those thugs to kill Shiva was Aditya Mehra!"

"I have a video," Ananya says, oddly calm, "Ashish mentioned that Rafiya might have the video yet, and she gave it to me three days ago."

"What nonsense are you saying!"

"*Papa,*" Ananya uses the same tone that he uses on her, the same soothing sound, "I think it was Sooraj. He is the one behind it; the murder, everything. He married me to get to the Chauhan family, and he implicated Aditya Mehra because he needed to ruin the Mehra family's reputation too. Two birds with one stone."

"Then what would he do, after getting into the Chauhan family?"

"God knows," Ananya throws up her hands, "I think Ashish knows the most. We need Ashish to talk about it."

"He's still at the hospital, Ananya."

"I found blood on Sooraj's shirt, on the night that Ashish had his accident, *papa*." Ananya says, in an effort to get her point across.

Her father stiffens.

"I don't know if he was the one who caused the accident, nor do I have any idea behind his motivations, but I know that he's involved. Somehow."

Dushyant Chauhan sits, head in his hands. It is the smallest that she has ever seen her father.

There is a knock, on Ananya's door. Once. Twice. Her mother.

Her father stands up, as if on autopilot, and opens the door, revealing a very distressed Damini Chauhan. Ananya's eyes widen. *I have never seen her like this, either.*

"It's Sooraj."

At the mention of her husband, Ananya turns sharply to her mother, "what happened to Sooraj?"

Her mother takes a few deep breaths, as if calming herself before the torm, "Sooraj was arrested by the police. Just an hour ago. For conspiracy to murder, as well as fraud."

Chapter 13

DUTY VS THE HEART

"Time is a created thing. To say 'I don't have time,' is like saying, 'I don't want to.'"

– Lao Tzu

This was perhaps her last court appearance. Ananya took a deep breath, before walking into the room. The first time that she had been here, it had been Aditya Mehra's trial, one that had ended half in disaster. This time, it was the trial of her own husband.

No, no longer her husband. The person who had her Shiva *Bhaiya* murdered, just to satisfy his thirst for revenge. She hadn't even known why Sooraj had been so hell-bent upon destroying her family, and she couldn't understand why they didn't want to tell her. Even to the end, her family would go on to keep secrets from her, would they?

"Witness for the prosecution, Ananya Rathi." The bailiff calls, and she stands, making her way to the stand. The wooden railings are sturdy enough to support her, and Ananya's knuckles are almost white, from gripping them too tightly.

"Mrs Rathi," the prosecutor, Mr Deshpande, begins after Ananya has taken her oath, "I am sure you are aware of your privilege as a spouse, are you?"

"Yes, I am," Ananya replies, "I do not have to disclose anything that my husband may have told me over the course of our marriage, as such conversations are exempt from being revealed in a court of law."

"Very well then. Please tell the court about the actions of Mr Rathi on the night of your brother's accident. 10th July, 2020. Where was your husband then?"

Ananya takes a deep breath. She was the final witness for the prosecution, a difficult position to be in.

"Mrs Rathi," Mr Deshpande begins, "what were you doing on the night of 10th July, 2020?"

Ananya takes a deep breath. "I was on the phone, talking to my brother, Ashish Chauhan. It was around ten at night, and my brother had called me on the phone."

"What was the conversation about?"

"He called me to say that Sooraj had visited the house that afternoon, and about the time that Sooraj and I met for the first time."

"And what did your brother say about your meeting with Mr Rathi?"

"He said that there was someone, who saw him paying Vikram Motwane, to introduce the two of us."

"And this person was?"

Ananya takes a deep breath. *Is this why people don't like being called to testify?* "The person who took the video was my brother's girlfriend."

Prosecutor Deshpande nods, before turning to the large screen set up in one corner of the courtroom, "play the recording."

Ananya has seen the video countless times, but even now, it sets her on edge—the shaky angle, and the conversation between them that could be clearly heard, "and what happened when he came home that night?"

"I found blood on his shirt." Ananya says.

There's a murmur around the courtroom.

"And the blood on his shirt matched the blood found in your brother's car, is that right?"

Ananya nods, "I gave the shirt as evidence to the police officers the next day, and the blood on it was a match to my brother's."

"That would be all, thank you."

Ananya heaves a sigh. She was not supposed to be this nervous. *It's only cross-examination.*

"Mrs Rathi," the defence lawyer, Mr Gupta, whom she knew very well, stands up next, "regarding the video of Mr Rathi with Aditya Mehra and Vikram Motwane, was the video taken by you?"

"No, sir. It was taken by Rafiya Ahmad, my brother's then-girlfriend." Ananya says. *Rafiya would forgive me, but Ashish won't.* "She took the video at *Divine.*"

"However, the bartender for that night, Akash, does not remember any such transaction taking place." Mr Gupta says, "so, Mrs Rathi, who is lying here, you or Ms Ahmad?"

"What do you mean?" Ananya almost shouts, "there were so many people that night at the club, its no wonder he doesn't remember!"

"Still, he was present there for the entire night, it is a wonder he does not remember."

"It isnt," Ananya mutters, "I don't remember meeting my husband either. The video is proof that he paid someone to do it."

"Mrs Rathi," Attorney Gupte leans in close, "don't you think that you're judging your husband carelessly? He could have been paying off a debt, or he may have just been lending Aditya Mehra money. Why do you think it was because of you that he paid Vikram Motwane money?"

"Why was his blood on my brother's car?" Ananya retorts, 'do you think I can understand anything?"

"Objection, your honour," the prosecutor stands up, "leading question."

"Sustained, but couldn't you have objected faster?" The judge waves a hand, "please don't go on tangents, either of you."

"That will be all, your honour."

Ananya shakes her head, a single tear falling out of the corner of her eye. *Why is my life turning out to be like this?*

☙◈❧

"Inspector Ramanujan," the prosecution begins, "what did you find out about the defendant at Hisar, Haryana?"

Inspector Ramanujan takes a moment to gather his thoughts, and says "Hisar is the ancestral home of both the Mehras and the Chauhans, as well as Mr Sooraj Rathi."

"Mr Rathi had written Hisar as his official residence at his first job, which was with Lata Diamonds."

"And how did you find this?" Prosecutor Deshpande asks, "how were you sure that Sooraj Rathi had been lying to the Chauhans?"

"He had initially not disclosed his ancestral address when he met Ananya Chauhan, and his previous position at Lata Jewellers had not brought him into contact with any of the executives, which helped him to fabricate his history. We would have never found out about his ancestral home if it had not been for the employee records that were found in Shiva Apte's laptop."

"So, Inspector Ramamanujan, what you mean to say is that Sooraj Rathi, the accused, had concealed his history from his fiancée and her whole family, but was caught by Shiva Apte?"

"Yes." Inspector Ramanujan finishes, "we didn't find any other names."

The court is silent. Inspector Ramanujan takes a quick look around the room. There is only an empty space opposite him, where the accused, Sooraj Rathi is supposed to be. However, Sooraj had not appeared yet. "In my opinion, Sooraj Rathi was being blackmailed by Shiva Apte."

"No personal opinions, please, Inspector," prosecutor Deshpande says, turning to the bench, "there have been systematic deposits made in Shiva Apte's bank account, in the six months that Ananya and Sooraj had been engaged. The money has been traced to an offshore bank account, opened under a false name from Mr Rathi's company."

"Sooraj Rathi needed to kill Shiva Apte, because his blackmail was getting in the way of his ultimate goal, which was to take Lata Jewellers for his own."

"Speculation." Mr Gupte calls out form his chair, "My lord, you cannot possible allow someone to speculate in court."

"Sustained." Judge Dubey waves a hand, "no speculation, Mr Deshpande. We aren't here for the final scene of a whodunit."

"Very well, then," Prosecutor Deshpande acquiesces, "did Shiva Apte try and blackmail Mr Rathi?"

"The emails between the two of them date back far longer than six months," Inspector Ramanujan says, "Shiva Apte did not blackmail him in the beginning. In fact, they were on very good terms, as evident rfom the emails."

"What makes you think the relationship had gone sour?" Prosecutor Deshpande asks the Inspector, "what made you come to that conclusion?"

"The money that Shiva Apte had received from Sooraj Rathi, had started being deposited into the account about six months ago. The emails that Shiva Apte exchanged with Sooraj Rathi also change their tone—" Inspector Ramanujan points towards the prosecutor, who turns a sheaf of paper over to the bench, "Shiva Apte wanted more money every month, and despite the revenue of Sooraj Rathi's company, it was becoming increasingly difficult to arrange for the money."

"What do you mean?" Prosecutor Deshpande asks, "Sooraj Rathi's consultancy firm is one of the fastest-growing in the city."

"A large overseas consulting firm recently opened its office in the city, which made Sooraj Rathi lose much of his business, practically overnight," Inspector Ramanujan replies, "his revenue has been falling steadily for the past quarter."

"And is that all?"

"No, not really. Shiva Apte was also blackmailing him because he had found out the true identity of Sooraj Rathis's parents." Inspector Ramanujan says, "and on the opposite side, Sooraj's face pales, a detail not unnoticed by the prosecutor, "six months ago, before the blackmail began, Shiva Apte went to Hisar for a week. After which he began to extort Rathi for money."

"No more questions, Your Honour," Prosecutor Deshpande says, walking away. Inspector Ramanujan remains silent.

Attorney Gupte steps forward.

"Would you consider the fact that the murder of Shiva Apte was done not on Sooraj Rathi's orders, but an independent action taken by Aditya Mehra?" Attorney Gupte asks, "the twenty-five lakhs did not come from Sooraj Rathi, it came from the bank account of Aditya Mehra."

"Aditya Mehra did order the murder of Shiva Apte," Inspector Ramanujan says, "but, we must remember that the money sent to Vikram Motwane for the act of murder itself, while yes, came from Aditya Mehra's bank account, it was deposited into the offshore account moments after the death of Apte, which would not have been possible, if not someone who was present there, had told Aditya Mehra. The only phone call made in the minutes after Apte's death, was not from the numbers of any family member, but from the number of Sooraj Rathi."

"How are you so sure?" Attorney Gupte asks, but Sooraj's face is pale, and the smile on Prosecutor Deshpande's face says a lot. Inspector Ramanujan shifts forward.

"Phone call records."

Chapter 14

CHOWDHURY

"A thing is not necessarily true because a man dies for it."

– Oscar Wilde

"So, you are the officer-in-charge of Hisar police station, are you, Officer Chowdhury?" Prosecutor Deshpande asks, walking closer to the witness stand, "how long have you worked there?"

"I was at Hisar since 1980," Officer Chowdhury replies, looking extremely nervous to be there, "I was a constable for the first fifteen years, and then I was promoted to officer-in-charge at the station."

"And you are set to retire this year, am I correct?" Prosecutor Deshpande asks.

"Yes, sir," Officer Chowdhury turns to the bench, "I will be retiring next month."

"Within the span of this year, did Shiva Apte ever come to you?" Prosecutor Deshpande asks, "his travel records show a trip made to Hisar, Haryana."

"He did," Officer Chowdhury replies, "he came to me for information on Sooraj Rathi, and—well, I didn't think it was important then, but for him, it was. He repeatedly asked me for information on it."

"What incident did Mr Apte ask you about?"

"Well, he asked me about the shootout that happened thirty years ago, at Hisar." Officer Chowdhury says, "but it was irrelevant to the actual reason for the enquiry. He wanted information on Sooraj Rathi, and was asking around the village, too, but he asked me about the shootout that happened between the Chauhans and the Mehras thirty years ago."

There is an uneasy sort of silence in the courtroom, punctuated only by the lazy sound of the rotating overhead fans, "what do you mean?" the judge asks, "the *shootout* between the Mehras and the Chauhans? Why is there no record of this?"

"We didn't have a record of anyone dying, so there could not be a proper case made then." Officer Chowdhury looks down at his hands, "Both Ravinder Mehra's father, who was the head of the Mehra family then, as well as Maan Singh Chauhan paid the police station bribes to hush up the incident."

"Maan Singh Chauhan?"

"Yes, Maan Singh Chauhan, the head of Lata Diamonds," Officer Chowdhury explains, "I was only a constable then, but later I learnt that there was someone who was fatally injured on that day. the hospitals did not have a record of them, which was probably why it did not appear on the report drawn up by the officer-in-charge then."

Judge Dubey stares at the man, "There was a murder and you did not report it?"

"The woman died in the hospital, about three weeks after the shooting, which was probably why the hospital did not report it to the police," Officer Chowdhury says, addressing the bench, "I had no idea that the woman had died due to the injuries she sustained in the incident."

"The post-mortem report," Prosecutor Deshpande holds up a file, "clearly said the woman died from burns."

"Despite it not being investigated, why was there no news of the skirmish or the gunshots in the local newspapers."

"Three days before the incident, there was a wedding in the village, and a wedding means a lot of celebration. That night, the gunshots were simply mistaken for celebratory fire."

Judge Dubey sighs, "and is there any reason why law enforcement allowed this to happen?"

"Sir," Officer Chowdhury seems slightly disturbed for revealing this, "sir, there is very little that we can do, even as police officers. Guns? Sure, we have them, but so do the people who are on the wrong side of the law."

"Officer Chowdhury," Prosecutor Deshpande cuts in, "could you please tell us the name of the woman who was murdered thirty years ago?"

"Sheela. Her name was Sheela, and her father's name was Rathi." Officer Chowdhury pauses, "I gave this information to Shiva Apte.

"Shiva Apte? And what did he do after receiving this information?"

"He told me something. Initially, I dismissed it, thinking that he was out of his mind, but as more time went by, I think even I was convinced by his argument. Shiva Apte was determined."

"Determined to do what?"

"He was sure that Sooraj Rathi was the son of Sheela Rathi. He even requested for the DNA samples of Sheela's postmortem report, but the technology was not sufficient yet to extract a sample, so he wasn't allowed to get one,"

"Allowed to?" prosecutor Deshpande asks, "Was Shiva Apte entitled to getting the DNA records of Sheela's child from her?"

"There wasn't any entitlement on the part of Shiva Apte," Officer Chowdhury says, regretfully, "although I could feel that he really needed the records, we could not hand it over to him because he was not family. The case had been closed, so we could have given him information, but as he was not family, we could not."

"He wasn't family, so all we could do was tell him things." Officer Chowdhury continues, "but I knew he was not the kind of person to just—give up."

"What makes you think that Shiva Apte actually found out about the truth of his assumption?" Prosecutor Deshpande asks, "did he have any sort of evidence regarding whether Sooraj Rathi may have been the child of the person killed in the 1990 incident?"

"He did speak to me," Officer Chowdhury replies, "he said that he had found out conclusive evidence. Forced DNA testing is illegal in India, but he was sure."

"So, he carried out DNA tests?" Prosecutor Deshpande asks, "without the knowledge of Sooraj Rathi?"

"Yes, but he did find out that Sheela Rathi's then one-year old sn was Sooraj Rathi," Officer Chowdhury explains, "he went to an orphanage, and he grew up under a different name."

"Which is why Shiva Apte found it difficult to track him down."

"He came back to me a few weeks before his death—saying that the son of Sheela Rathi had changed his name after he had turned eighteen, and was now successful in his own right." Officer Chowdhury replies, "Shiva Apte told me that he recognised the boy because he had changed his name back to his mother's maiden name."

"His mother's maiden name was Rathi? Was she not married when she had him?"

"She was unmarried, or had no registered spouse." Officer Chowdhury shrugs, "it's not an uncommon occurrence where I am from."

"He tracked his mother down?" Prosecutor Deshpande asks, "he must not have been older than a few years when his mother was murdered."

"He changed his name to Sooraj Rathi when he turned eighteen," Officer Chowdhury says, pointing at Sooraj, who had been standing quietly, until now, "Shiva Apte went to the orphanage where Sheela Rathi's son had grown up, and found out that he had changed his name to his mother's maiden one."

The courtroom is again plunged into silence, an uneasy one, punctuated by the harsh breaths taken by Sooraj on the stand, "you can't prove any of that bullshit."

"What?" Prosecutor Deshpande turns, "what did you say?"

"Shiva apte is dead," Sooraj says, the ends of his mouth curving upwards in a smile, "you're putting so much trust in the words of a dead man, when you can't even verify anything. All you are going off is the statement given by a police officer, who already admitted to being corrupt? Who's to say that he hadn't taken a bribe from someone? Or promised something in return for incriminating me?"

"Mr Rathi, might I say that this could be construed as contempt of court?" Judge Dubey says, "do you really wish to be held and tried for that offence, along with the many that you are currently on trial for?"

"Will that make a difference?" Sooraj says, and Judge Dubey brings down the gavel, "Order in my court! Mr Rathi, one more word, and I will hold you in contempt of the court. Prosecutor Deshpande, might I suggest that speculating about someone's criminal origins might be best left to the reporters and the theorists?"

"Apologies, your honour," Prosecutor Deshpande says, before turning back to Officer Chowdhury, "of all that you have alleged against the defendant, do you have any direct evidence that related him to Sheela Rathi? Or anything that indicated that he may be tied to the case?"

"Shiva Apte's laptop." Officer Chowdhury replies, "Shiva Apte had everything on his laptop. Documented. He would have the documents regarding the orphanage, as well as Sooraj Rathi's change of last name, everything organised on there."

ॐ◆ॐ

"Mr Mehra," Prosecutor Deshpande says, "what a pleasant surprise to see you here, on this side of the defence."

Aditya Mehra doesn't say anything, simply scowls in response. *What would he say?* His father, well, Ravinder Mehra, had ensured that Aditya would never be able to make a living for himself, at least if he remained in Delhi. Or even in India. The drug charges were one thing, but Aditya has a feeling that this time, he had stumbled into something much larger than himself, or even his whole family.

There were newspapers in judicial custody. Something that Aditya had never really thought of, but there were newspapers in judicial custody. And all that the papers could tlak about, were the surprising revelations of the city's top diamond merchant's daughter being involved with someone whose family—well, it didn't really exist, did it—never really existed in the first place. There were pictures of Ananya Chauhan too, shellshocked and heartbroken at the news of her husband becoming a murderer. Aditya Mehra found himself sympathising with her at times. Being betrayed by someone one trusted—it was never easy. Not for him, and certainly not for Ananya.

On the opposte end of the courtroom, Sooraj Rathi stands, and Aditya Mehra has to pause, only for a moment, to look at the man who was, until a few weeks ago, on the top of the world. *Can you imagine?* Married to the Chauhan's daughter, with his own successful firm, and now—now he has nothing.

"Mr Aditya Mehra," Prosecutor Deshpande says, tone considerably lighter than what Aditya had been subjected to at his own trial, "did you have any contact with the defendant over the past year?"

"Yes, I did," Aditya says, "I thought I gave my statement to the police officers."

"This is for the sake of the court, Mr Mehra," Prosecutor Deshpande remarks, "when did you meet Sooraj Rathi? Under what circumstances?"

Aditya sighs. He really did not want to do this to Sooraj. After all, the man had been helpful to him, and Aditya wasn't a child. He knew what he was doing, the implications of the actions that he had done.

"I met Sooraj Rathi at the club, *Divine,* couple years ago," Aditya says, "we were both at a party for a film premiere. He introduced himself as a consultant on the film. Of course, I knew that probably was not true, but I didn't care very much. He seemed to be a good person."

"What happened after that?" Prosecutor Deshpande asks, "when did you start colluding with Sooraj Rathi?"

"About a year ago," Aditya replies, "my father had been thinking of retiring, and I knew that he would never leave the family business to me. or have anything to do with me, even. So, I said all this to Sooraj, and he proposed that we should take down Lata Diamonds, a move that would make my father more appreciative of me."

Aditya hangs his head. What he had done, while not a split-second decision, was not made on the spur of the moment either. He had knownt hat this was going to happen, sooner or later.

"So, you wanted to destroy Lata Diamonds, but why ask Shiva Apte to be a part of your scheme?"

Aditya takes a moment to reply, "you know, they didn't treat Shiva well, either."

"Sure, they all called him Shiva-*bhaiya* and went around telling people that he was a pillar of their company, but in reality, Shiva was just someone they were taking advantage of. He did all the work, and they never even acknowledged him for it."

"In the last year, the CEO of Lata Diamonds, Anshul Chauhan, had a salary of three crores." Prosecutor Deshpande says, "was Mr Apte dissatisfied?"

"Anshul Chauhan barely even went down to the manufacturing plants, and yet he had the largest salary cut out fo anyone in that company," Aditya replies to the question, "Shiva Apte was the one who did all the work. He was the one who went to the manufacturers, finalised the designs, and paid the craftsmen. He did everything, and the Chauhans knew it. Anshul Chauhan knew it, and he never acknowledged Shiva Apte's efforts." Aditya finds his own voice rising, "he wanted his efforts to be recognised. Which is why he sought me out."

"Shiva Apte sought you out?" Prosecutor Deshpande is shocked, although half of it's an act, "he didn't seek out Sooraj Rathi?"

"I introduced him to Sooraj," Aditya says, "I told Shiva Apte that it would be a good idea, to take down Lata Diamonds from the inside. Shiva was not being respected, and sooraj took advantage of that. He took advantage of the both of us, I know, but yes. I introduced Shiva Apte to Sooraj Rathi, and now Shiva Apte is dead."

"What caused the difference of opinions and the subsequent falling out between Shiva Apte and Sooraj Rathi?"

"Shiva went to Hisar a few months ago, and when he returned, he immediately went to see Sooraj," Aditya sayas, recounting what had happened over six months ago, "and I remember being in the room with Sooraj when Shiva Apte entered the room, still with the suitcase that he had taken with him to Hisar, and I remember them arguing over it."

There had been words exchanged, sharp words, words that Aditya had not really heard very well, behind closed doors, "I did not hear what they were saying, but after that. Shiva Apte stopped meeting both me and Sooraj. He even stopped sending us information about the business dealings of Lata diamonds."

"Shiva Apte sent you confidential information about the business dealings of Lata diamonds?"

"Yes, yes, he did. He said that he had felt disposable throughout his life, and that by getting back at Lata Diamonds and the Chauhan family for what they did to him throughout his life, he would gain self-satisfaction, at least."

"He said that?" Judge Dubey asks, "the files on Shiva Apte's laptop, the ones that we recovered, contained information about Lata Diamnds, and its day-to-day dealings, but he turned over all that to you?"

"Yes, your Honour, the emails that we have recovered from Aditya Mehra's computer, as well as the conversation between him and Shiva Apte, can lead us to reasonably think that there was an exchange of information happening, sensitive information, regarding the business dealings of Lata diamonds."

"The increased market share of Mehra Jewellery is not a coincidence," Aditya says, "there are very few people who know about it, but I gave my father all the information that he needed, in order to overtake Lata Diamonds in the market share."

"And he did, but six months ago, the reports started becoming scarce, am I correct?" Prosecutor Deshpande asks, "Shiva Apte refused to have anything to do with the son of someone who's family had been torn apart because of the Chauhans and the Mehras. Should he not have renounced the Chauhan family instead of abandoning Sooraj Rathi?"

"Sooraj asked him to leave, and that is all I know of their exchange," Aditya replies, "I met Shiva Apte four months ago. He knew that Sooraj was not happy with him meddling in Sooraj's private affairs, so I told him politely, to maybe apologise to Sooraj."

"And what did he say?"

"He told me to keep myself safe, and not to worry about him," Aditya replies to the question "Prosecutor—I mean, Your Honour, Shiva Apte did not have to die. He was prepared for it, but he did not have to die."

"What makes you think that he was prepared to die?" Prosecutor Deshapande asks, "did Shiva Apte tell you that his death was imminent?"

"He told me that he was getting his affairs in order." Aditya replies, "I think he was planning to retire from the job, because all he could talk about was Ananya's wedding. I knew he was excited for it."

"Did he say anything about Ananya's fiancé?"

"No, he did not, which was a bit strange, since we both knew that Ananya was going to marry Sooraj Rathi." Aditya finishes, "after all, he paid me and Vikram to introduce him to her."

"He did?"

"He did," Aditya replies, "he met Ananya at the same nightclub where I met him, *Divine*."

"And what do you remember of Shiva Apte's death?"

Aditya takes a deep breath. Opposite him, at the defendant's dock, Sooraj Rathi stands, as proud as ever, apparently, because even the prospect of going to prison for most of his life did not seem to daunt Sooraj Rathi. He still had the same tilt to his mouth, and Aditya wants to turn away, but he cannot, not really. All his life, he had been running, so for once, he would like to meet this, head-on. Like a person. Not as a coward.

"Shiva Apte had called Sooraj Rathi, the week before their engagement party, and the two of them exchanged words. I remember Shiva Apte calling Sooraj a 'bastard', but I may have heard wrong. And then Sooraj turned to me, and told me to make the problem go away."

"He asked you to make the problem go away?" Judge Dubey asks, "anf you had Shiva Apte murdered?"

"I simply paid the person in concern," Aditya says, "I was nothing more than the middleman in this operation. The idea was entirely Sooraj's. he planned to take Ananya to a drive, in order to distract him from the happenings of her family, and the incident at her house."

"I paid Vikram Motwane with the money that Sooraj Rathi wired to me," Aditya continues, "I do not think Sooraj expected to be caught."

"No more questions, your honour," Prosecutor Deshpande walks off, and Attorney Gupte takes his place.

"Mr Mehra, would you classify your hearing as excellent?" the defence attorney asks, "how were you so sure about what argument Shiva Apte and Sooraj Rathi had?"

"I was at the Chauhan residence that afternoon," Aditya Mehra replies, "and the argument that occurred, took place over the landline. I xould hear everything clearly."

"Wouldn't Shiva Apte's death also benefit you, Mr Mehra?" Attorney Gupte asks, "you yourself told that you were becoming unsatisfied with the treatment that you face, at your father's hands. Shiva Apte's death meant a look at the files on his laptop, files, which would help you and your family to overtake the Chauhans in market share."

"It did not really make sense for him to die because of that, sir," Aditya replies, "why would I murder Shiva Apte, and run the risk of the police getting to know, and the eventual publicity storm, when I could just leave it alone?"

Chapter 15

THE WITNESS

"There is nothing either good or bad, but thinking
makes it so."

– William Shakespeare, Hamlet

"State your name for the record, please."

"My name is Rafiya Ahmad."

"Where did you see the accused, and when?"

"At *Divine*, the club. I went there only once, but I knew
them from the tabloids. Even if you didn't peruse the pages,
you knew who they were."

"Who?"

"The socialites. They were always on the front pages.
Aditya Mehra and his cousin—Vikram Motwane, were both
like that. With a new girl on every arm. For every occasion. I
knew them from the papers."

"Who else did you see that night?"

"I was with no one, but I saw Ananya Chauhan, with her
friends," Rafiya says softly, "I remember she was a big help to
me at the time, so, I thought of going over and introducing
myself, but before I could, the alcohol and the drugs kicked
in, and I felt very light-headed."

"Drugs?"

"Yes, which is why I had to lie down on one of the sofas. I was not high, I was drunk, which was why I wanted to be on there on a short period of time."

"What did you see?"

"I never saw Sooraj offering money to anybody else, so I presumed that he knew them both. Then I started recording, because I saw something really funny that was happening at that moment, but then the three of them are now in the background of my video, and Sooraj is giving Vikram Motwane money."

"Who did you send this to?"

"Ashish Mehra. He told me that I should let him go. We were in a relationship, and we broke up. After that, I had some news rhat was upsetting to me, so I went to the club to de-stress. That is the only time that I have been at that club."

"Is that all that happened?"

"After Sooraj began chatting up Ananya, I tried to leave, but someone drugged me, and I woke up at the hospital. A girl I know had taken me to the hospital, and they told me that I had almost died of an accidental overdose."

"Do you know who drugged your drink?"

"The club could not find the person who did that, so they simply told me to be more careful from then on, and sent me home."

❦◈❧

"Mr Rathi," Prosecutor Deshpande says, "where were you on the night of the murder of Shiva Apte?"

"I was on a drive with my then-fiancee, Annaya Chauhan," Sooraj replies, "I don't see why this is of any significance."

"Mr Rathi, would you explain the nature of your correspondence with Shiva Apte and Aditya Mehra?"

"There was no communication. I never talked to either Shiva Apte, or Aditya Mehra."

"Witness statements put you in the vicinity of the two of them,in the beginning of this year," Prosecutor Deshpande holds up a granny picture, obviously enhanced, "this is you with the two of them, having a 'casual' lunch at the Marriott hotel, right, Mr Rathi?"

"So, I may have had a lunch with them," Sooraj shrugs, "still does not prove anything."

"No, it does not. But the transactions made from your bank account to Mr Apte's, make a lot more sense, don't they? Not to mention the money that went from your account to the offshore one held in Aditya Mehra's name. the paper trail says something else entirely, Mr Rathi. Sure, you used a bank account under your mother's name, but the activity can be traced directly to you."

"Shiva Apte blackmailing me, does not mean that I killed him. yes, he did blackmail me, and yes, I paid him the money, but I never murdered him!"

"No, Mr Rathi," Prosecutor Deshpande replies, "but with Aditya Mehra's testimony, there is a credible enough case against you."

Sooraj doesn't say anything. *This was not supposed to go this way. My revenge was supposed to be easy, efficient. Lethal. I wanted to destroy the two of them, and now, now I'm caught in the crosshairs.*

"Mr Rathi," Prosecutor Deshpande says, "are you Sheela Rathi's son?"

Chapter 16

THE HOUSE

"We know what we are, but not what we may be."

– William Shakespeare

"So, what is going to happen now?" Ashish asks, lying down on the bed, "both Mehra Jewellery and Lata Diamonds seem to be doing badly. There is no reason for us to remain in the company anymore."

"No, *bhaiya*," Ananya replies, holding her brother's hand, "you should go take a holiday. I'll take care of matters on our end."

⊰◈⊱

"Sir, the Chauhans and the Mehras won't be prosecuted for what happened in Hisar thirty years ago, will they?" Deputy Inspector Alam asks, picking up a paperweight, "I can't imagine killing someone over something as trivial as a wedding gone wrong."

"It was more than just the wedding, Alam," Inspector Ramanujan replies, "the Mehra's had their daughter engaged to the eldest son of the Chauhan family. This was a merger, not a love marriage. And three days before the wedding, Anshul Chauhan ran away with the daughter of their steward, Kamala. The Mehras were angry, and the Chauhans were defensive. In the middle of it, Sheela Rahti lost her life, and her one-year-old son, grew up without a mother, or a father."

"Sooraj Rathi did manage to get his revenge after all," Deputy Inspector Alam picks up a newspaper, "the market share of both Mehra Jewellery and Lata Diamonds is going down rapidly, from the day of the final hearing."

"I hadn't seen that," Inspector Ramanujan replies, picking up the paper from Deputy Inspector Alam's hands, "well, they both had it coming. Maan Singh Chauhan began his life as a smuggler, and then after getting rich, he tried to become a legitimate businessman."

"Maan Singh Chauhan, a smuggler?" Deputy Inspector Alam says, confused, "but if he were a smuggler, that means he—"

"He was one of the people the Haryana police did not manage to catch, smuggling drugs across the border to Punjab, and even Pakistan. Heroin, cocaine, marijuana, you name it, he had a hand in the pot. We couldn't catch him after so long, because there's barely any evidence left. In the seventies, he retired, leaving the business to his older sons, Anshul and Angad."

"But they were landowners in Hisar."

"Of course, they were. They cultivated poppy." Inspector Ramanujan says, wry smile in place, "Alam, you should really begin to go out and talk to the witnesses more. The farmers in Hisar all confirmed the same thing, that they were growing poppy for both the Mehra family and the Chauhan family, as well as the supposed wedding between the oldest daughter of the Mehras, Chandni, and the oldest son of the Chauhans, Anshul. However, Anshul ran off with Kamala, the daughter of their steward, three days before the wedding was scheduled to take place."

"And the Mehras were humiliated." Deputy Inspector Alam finishes, "which led to the shootout."

"There was more than just a shootout. Someone lit acres of poppy fields on fire. The estimated loss was in lakhs, in 1990." Inspector Ramanujan picks up a paper from the folder lying on top of the table, "after this, the Chauhan family shifted to Delhi, and the Mehras followed suit. Their bitter rivalry was actually from past history, not just professional."

"Who began the shootout at Hisar?" Deputy Inspector Alam asks, "Maan Singh was retired back then, and he wouldn't be so stupid as to start a whole turf war. The point of the marriage was a merger."

"Ravinder Mehra's father, Arjun Mehra had only passed away three months before the shooting," Inspector Ramanujan points at the line written on the paper, "Ravinder was only thirty at the time. No children, and hot-headed too. He took it upon himself to avenge his sister's honour."

"Honour." Deputy Inspector Alam repeats, "why is it that families like these have such a skewed idea of it?"

"You tell me, Alam," Inspector Ramanujan replies, "what's happening to Aditya Mehra?"

"He's the government witness against Sooraj Rathi, and also against the case of illegal gold mining, against both Lata Diamonds, and Mehra Jewellery," Deputy Inspector Alam picks up the newspaper, "it's not on the papers yet, but it will be. Shiva Apte gave Aditya Mehra all the documents that we needed to bring a case against the Chauhans, and Aditya himself provided the rest of the evidence to indict the Mehras."

"Damn. He's only a kid, you know," Inspector Ramanujan says, "I hope the kids live well. Ashish Chauhan has gone off to Europe, and Ananya Chauhan will take over the family business. I think she'll dismantle the company."

"Poetic justice, should we call it?"

"You seem to have an overactive imagination, Alam," Inspector Ramanujan says, "Sooraj Rathi got life imprisonment. Twelve years, and Shiva Apte lost his life. Come on, Alam, let's go."

"Where, sir?" Deputy Inspector Alam runs after his superior, picking up a folder from the table, "sir! You left this!"